THE DAYS
RUN AWAY
LIKE WILD
HORSES OVER
THE HILLS
CHARLES
BUKOWSKI

ecco

An Imprint of HarperCollinsPublishers

HarperCollins books maybe purchased for educational, business, or sales promotional use. For information, please e-mail the Special Markets Department at SPsales@harpercollins.com.

ACKNOWLEDGMENTS

Grateful acknowledgment to the editors of the following magazines, where some of these poems first apeared:
Ante, Avalanche, Caterpillar, Compass Review, Choice, Coastlines, Coffin, Dare, Dust, Earth, Epos, Evergreen Review, Evidence, Gallows, Grist, Harlequin, Hearst, Hiram Poetry Review, Iconolatre, Intrepid, Klatoveedsedsteen, Literary Artpress, Merlin's Magic, The New Lantern Club Review, Nomad, Northwest Review, Notes from Underground, Ole, Outcry, The Outsider, Oyez, Prism International, Quagga, Quicksilver, Quixote, Renaissance, Satis, Sciamachy, Semina, Showcase, Some/Thing, Southern Poetry Review, Stony Brook, Targets, Vagabond, Wild Dog, The Wormwood Review.

Some of these poems were also collected in the following chapbooks:
Flower, Fist and Bestial Wail (E. V. Griffith, editor & publisher, Hearse Chapbooks)
Poems and Drawings (Will Tullos & Evelyn Thorne, editors, Epos)
Longshot Pomes for Broke Players (Carl Larsen, editor & publisher, 7 Poets Press)
Run with the Hunted (R. R. Cuscaden, editor & publisher, Midwest Poetry Chapbooks)
Cold Dogs in the Courtyard (Jay Nash, editor & publisher, Literary Times-Cyfoeth)
A Bukowski Sampler (Morris Edelson, publisher, Quixote Press)

Library of Congress Cataloging-in-Publication Data has been applied for.

ISBN: 0-87685-006-9 (hc)
ISBN: 0-87685-005-0 (pbk)

23 24 25 26 27 LBC 29 28 27 26 25

for
Jane

Table of Contents

I.

II.

III.

I

get your name in LIGHTS
get it up there in
8½ x 11 mimeo

what a man I was

I shot off his left ear
then his right,
and then tore off his belt buckle
with hot lead,
and then
I shot off everything that counts
and when he bent over
to pick up his drawers
and his marbles
(poor critter)
I fixed it so he wouldn't have
to straighten up
no more.

Ho Hum.
I went in for a fast snort
and one guy *seemed*
to be looking at me sideways,
and that's how he died—
sideways,
lookin' at me
and clutchin'
for his marbles.

Sight o' blood made me kinda
hungry.
Had a ham sandwich.
Played a couple of sentimental songs . . .
Shot out all the lights
and strolled outside.
Didn't seem to be no one around

so I shot my horse
(poor critter).

Then I saw the Sheerf
a standin' at the end a' the road
and he was shakin'
like he had the Saint Vitus dance;
it was a real sorrowful sight
so I slowed him to a quiver
with the first slug
and mercifully stiffened him
with the second.

Then I laid on my back awhile
and I shot out the stars one by one
and then
I shot out the moon
and then I walked around
and shot out every light
in town,
and pretty soon it began to get dark
real dark
the way I like it;
just can't stand to sleep
with no light shinin'
on my face.

I laid down and dreamt
I was a little boy again
a playin' with my toy six-shooter
and winnin' all the marble games,
and when I woke up
my guns was gone
and I was all bound hand and foot
just like somebody
was scared a me

and they was slippin'
a noose around my ugly neck
just as if they
meant to hang me,
and some guy was pinnin'
a real pretty sign
on my shirt:
there's a law for you
and a law for me
and a law that hangs
from the foot of a tree.

Well, pretty poetry always did
make my eyes water
and can you believe it
all the women was cryin'
and though they was moanin'
other men's names
I just know they was cryin'
for me (poor critters)
and though I'd slept with all a them,
I'd forgotten
in all the big excitement
to tell 'em my name

and all the men looked angry
but I guess it was because the kids
was all being impolite
and a throwin' tin cans at me,
but I told 'em not to worry
because their aim was bad anyhow
not a boy there looked like he'd turn
into a man—
90% homosexuals, the lot of them,
and some guy shouted
"let's send him to hell!"

and with a jerk I was dancin'
my last dance,
but I swung out wide
and spit in the bartender's eye
and stared down
into Nellie Adam's breasts,
and my mouth watered again.

mine

She lays like a lump
I can feel the great empty mountain
of her head.
But she is alive. She yawns and
scratches her nose and
pulls up the cover.
Soon I will kiss her goodnight
and we will sleep.
and far away is Scotland
and under the ground the
gophers run.
I hear engines in the night
and through the sky a white
hand whirls:
good night, dear, goodnight.

freedom

he drank wine all night the night of the
28th. and he kept thinking of her:
the way she walked and talked and loved
the way she told him things that seemed true
but were not, and he knew the color of each
of her dresses
and her shoes—he knew the stock and curve of
each heel
as well as the leg shaped by it.

and she was out again when he came home, and
she'd come back with the special stink again,
and she did
she came in at 3 a.m. in the morning
filthy like a dung-eating swine
and
he took out the butcher knife
and she screamed
backing into the roominghouse wall
still pretty somehow
in spite of love's reek
and he finished the glass of wine.

that yellow dress
his favorite
and she screamed again.

and he took up the knife
and unhooked his belt
and tore away the cloth before her
and cut off his balls.

and carried them in his hands
like apricots
and flushed them down the
toilet bowl
and she kept screaming
as the room became red

GOD O GOD!
WHAT HAVE YOU DONE?

and he sat there holding 3 towels
between his legs
not caring now whether she left or
stayed
wore yellow or green or
anything at all.

and one hand holding and one hand
lifting he poured
another wine.

as the sparrow

To give life you must take life,
and as our grief falls flat and hollow
upon the billion-blooded sea
I pass upon serious inward-breaking shoals rimmed
with white-legged, white-bellied rotting creatures
lengthily dead and rioting against surrounding scenes.
Dear child, I only did to you what the sparrow
did to you; I am old when it is fashionable to be
young; I cry when it is fashionable to laugh.
I hated you when it would have taken less courage
to love.

his wife, the painter

There are sketches on the walls of men and women and
        ducks,
and outside a large green bus swerves through traffic like
insanity sprung from a waving line; Turgenev, Turgenev,
says the radio, and Jane Austen, Jane Austen, too.

"I am going to do her portrait on the 28th, while you are
at work."

He is just this edge of fat and he walks constantly, he
fritters; they have him; they are eating him hollow like
a webbed fly, and his eyes are red-suckled with anger-fear.

He feels the hatred and discard of the world, sharper than
his razor, and his gut-feel hangs like a wet polyp; and he
self-decisions himself defeated trying to shake his
hung beard from razor in water (like life), not warm enough.

Daumier. Rue Transnonain, le 15 Avril, 1843. (Lithograph.)
Paris, Bibliotheque Nationale.

"She has a face unlike that of any woman I have ever
        known."

"What is it? A love affair?"

"Silly. I can't love a woman. Besides, she's pregnant."

I can paint—a flower eaten by a snake; that sunlight is a
lie; and that markets smell of shoes and naked boys clothed,
and under everything some river, some beat, some twist that

clambers along the edge of my temple and bites
     nip-dizzy . . .
men drive cars and paint their houses,
but they are mad; men sit in barber chairs; buy hats.

Corot. Recollection of Mortefontaine.
Paris, Louvre.

"I must write Kaiser, though I think he's a homosexual."

"Are you still reading Freud?"

"Page 299."

She made a little hat and he fastened two snaps under one
arm, reaching up from the bed like a long feeler from the
snail, and she went to church, and he thought now I h've
time and the dog.

About church: the trouble with a mask is it
never changes.

So rude the flowers that grow and do not grow beautiful.
So magic the chair on the patio that does not hold legs
and belly and arm and neck and mouth that bites into the
wind like the end of a tunnel.

He turned in bed and thought: I am searching for some
segment in the air. It floats about the people's heads.
When it rains on the trees it sits between the branches
warmer and more blood-real than the dove.

Orozco. Christ Destroying the Cross.
Hanover, Dartmouth College, Baker Library.

He burned away in sleep.

down thru the marching

they came down thru the marching,
down thru St. Paul, St. Louis, Atlanta,
Memphis, New Orleans, they came
down thru the marching, thru
balloons and popcorn, past drugstores
and blondes and whirling cats,
they came down thru the marching
scaring the goats and the kids in
the fields, banging against the minds
of the sick in their hot beds, and
down in the cellar I got out the
colt. I ripped a hole in the screen
for better vision and when the legs
came walking by on top of my head,
I got a colonel, a major and 3 lieutenants
before the band stopped playing;
and now it's like a war, uniforms
everywhere, behind cars and brush,
and plang plang plang
my cellar is all fireworks, and I
fire back, the colt as hot as a
baked potato, I fire back and sing
sing, "Mine eyes have seen the glory
of the coming of the Lord; He is
tramping out the vintage . . ."

these things

these things that we support most well
have nothing to do with us,
and we do with them
out of of boredom or fear or money
or cracked intelligence;
our circle and our candle of light
being small,
so small we cannot bear it,
we heave out with Idea
and lose the Center:
all wax without the wick,
and we see names that once meant wisdom,
like signs into ghost towns,
and only the graves are real.

poem for personnel managers:

An old man asked me for a cigarette
and I carefully dealt out two.
"Been lookin' for job. Gonna stand
in the sun and smoke."

He was close to rags and rage
and he leaned against death.
It was a cold day, indeed, and trucks
loaded and heavy as old whores
banged and tangled on the streets . . .

We drop like planks from a rotting floor
as the world strives to unlock the bone
that weights its brain.
(God is a lonely place without steak.)

We are dying birds
we are sinking ships—
the world rocks down against us
and we
throw out our arms
and we
throw out our legs
like the death kiss of the centipede:
but they kindly snap our backs
and call our poison "politics."

Well, we smoked, he and I—little men
nibbling fish-head thoughts . . .

All the horses do not come in,
and as you watch the lights of the jails
and hospitals wink on and out,
and men handle flags as carefully as babies,
remember this:

you are a great-gutted instrument of
heart and belly, carefully planned—
so if you take a plane for Savannah,
take the best plane;
or if you eat chicken on a rock,
make it a very special animal.
(You call it a bird; I call birds
flowers.)

And if you decide to kill somebody,
make it anybody and not somebody:
some men are made of more special, precious
parts: do not kill
if you will
a president or a King
or a man
behind a desk—
these have heavenly longitudes
enlightened attitudes.

If you decide,
take us
who stand and smoke and glower;
we are rusty with sadness and
feverish
with climbing broken ladders.

Take us:
        we were never children
        like your children.

We do not understand love songs
like your inamorata.

Our faces are cracked linoleum,
cracked through with the heavy, sure
feet of our masters.

We are shot through with carrot tops
and poppyseed and tilted grammar;
we waste days like mad blackbirds
and pray for alcoholic nights.
Our silk-sick human smiles wrap around
us like somebody else's confetti:
we do not even belong to the Party.

We are a scene chalked-out with the
sick white brush of Age.

We smoke, asleep as a dish of figs.
We smoke, dead as a fog.

Take us.

A bathtub murder
or something quick and bright; our names
in the papers.

Known, at last, for a moment
to millions of careless and grape-dull eyes
that hold themselves private
to only flicker and flame
at the poor cracker-barrel jibes
of their conceited, pampered correct comedians.

Known, at last, for a moment,
as they will be known

and as you will be known
by an all-gray man on an all-gray horse
who sits and fondles a sword
longer than the night
longer than the mountain's aching backbone
longer than all the cries
that have a-bombed up out of throats
and exploded in a newer, less-planned
land.

We smoke and the clouds do not notice us.
A cat walks by and shakes Shakespeare off of his back.
Tallow, tallow, candle like wax: our spines
are limp and our consciousness burns
guilelessly away
the remaining wick life has
doled out to us.

An old man asked me for a cigarette
and told me his troubles
and this
is what he said:
that Age was a crime
and that Pity picked up the marbles
and that Hatred picked up the
cash.

He might have been your father
or mine.

He might have been a sex-fiend
or a saint.

But whatever he was,
he was condemned
and we stood in the sun and

smoked
and looked around
in our leisure
to see who was next in
line.

ice for the eagles

I keep remembering the horses
under the moon
I keep remembering feeding the horses
sugar
white oblongs of sugar
more like ice,
and they had heads like
eagles
bald heads that could bite and
did not.

The horses were more real than
my father
more real than God
and they could have stepped on my
feet but they didn't
they could have done all kinds of horrors
but they didn't.

I was almost 5
but I have not forgotten yet;
o my god they were strong and good
those red tongues slobbering
out of their souls.

plea to a passing maid

girl in shorts, biting your nails, revolving your ass,
the boys are looking at you—
                              you hold more, it seems,
than Gauguin or Brahma or Balzac,
more, at least, than the skulls that swim at our feet,
your swagger breaks the Eiffel tower,
turns the heads of old newsboys long ago gone
sexually to pot;
your caged malarkey, your idiot's dance,
mugging it, delightful—don't ever wash stained under-
wear or chase your acts of love
through neighborhood alleys—
don't spoil it for us,
putting on weight and weariness,
settling for TV and a namby-pamby husband;
don't give up that absurd dispossessed wiggle
to water a Saturday's front lawn—
don't send us back to Balzac or introspection
or Paris
or wine, don't send us back
to the incubation of our doubts or the memory
of death-wiggle, bitch, madden us with love
and hunger, keep the sharks, the bloody sharks,
from the heart.

waste basket

spoor and anemia and deviltry
and what can we make of this?:
a belly in the trash . . .
down by Mr. Saunders' beer cans
curled up like a cat;
life can be no less ludicrous
than rain
and as I take the lift
up to 3
I pass Mrs. Swanson
in the grate
powdered and really dead
but walking on
buying sweets and fats
and mailing Christmas cards;
and opening the door to my room
a fat damsel scrambles my vision
bottles fall
and a voice says
why are all your poems
personal?

: : : *the old movies*

          were best, the French F. Legion
every man with a bitch and the Arabs charging down
on white parade ponies, and the Sarge't holding the
fort by propping up dead men until re'forcemnts arriv'l.
And the ones with the boys flying around in the Spads
full of wire and one plat. blonde who seemed to symbolize
everything. Maybe it was just because I was a kid
or maybe it isn't the same any more. All the angles,
the cautious patriots, the air-raid wardens, cigarettes
for sex, and even the enemy seeming to play a game.
Or the time they found the Jap nurse in the shell-hole
who had been hit in the breast and wanted some sulfa
and one of the boys said, "Hey, you think we can fuck
her before she dies?"

peace

I thought the dove was the bird of peace
but here they were shooting them out
of the brush
and climbing up the sides of mountains
and banging them down;
and everywhere the doves went
there were the hunters
blasting and beaming and blasting,
and one man who didn't
in the slightest
resemble a dove
was shot in the shoulder;
and there were many complaints
that the doves
were smaller and scarcer
than last year,
but the way they fell
through the air
when you stung the life
out of them
was the same;
and I was there too
but I couldn't shoot anything
with a paintbrush;
and a couple of them
came over to my canvas
and stood and stood and stood
until I finally said,
for God's sake
go look at Picasso and Rembrandt,
go look at Klee and Gauguin,

listen to a symphony by Mahler,
and if you get anything
out of that
come back
and stare at my canvas!

what the hell's wrong with
him? the one guy
said.

he's nuts. they're all nuts,
the other guy said. anyhow,
I got my 10 doves.

me too, his buddy said, let's
go home: we can have them
in the pan
by 2:30.

I taste the ashes of your death

the blossoms shake
sudden water
down my sleeve,
sudden water
cool and clean
as snow—
as the stem-sharp
swords
go in
against your breast
and the sweet wild
rocks
leap over
and
lock us in.

for Jane: with all the love I had,
which was not enough:—

I pick up the skirt,
I pick up the sparkling beads
in black,
this thing that moved once
around flesh,
and I call God a liar,
I say anything that moved
like that
or knew
my name
could never die
in the common verity of dying,
and I pick
up her lovely
dress,
all her loveliness gone,
and I speak
to all the gods,
Jewish gods, Christ-gods,
chips of blinking things,
idols, pills, bread,
fathoms, risks,
knowledgeable surrender,
rats in the gravy of 2 gone quite mad
without a chance,
hummingbird knowledge, hummingbird chance,
I lean upon this,
I lean on all of this
and I know:

her dress upon my arm:
but
they will not
give her back to me.

Uruguay or hell

it should have been Mexico
she always liked Mexico
and Arizona and New Mexico
and tacos,
but not the flies
and so there I was
standing there—
durable
visible
clothed
waiting.

the priest was angry:
he had been arguing with the boy
for several days
over his mother's right to have a
Catholic burial
and they finally settled
that it could not be in
church
but he would say the
thing at the grave.
the priest cared about
technicalities
the son did not care
except about the
bill.

I was the
lover

and I cared but what I cared for
was dead.

there were just 3 of
us: son,
landlady,
lover. it was
hot. the priest waved his words
in the air and
then he was
done. I walked to the
priest and thanked him for the
words.
and we walked
off
we got into the car
we drove away.

it should have been Mexico
or Uruguay or hell.
the son let me out at my
place and said he'd write me about a
stone but I knew he was lying—
that if there was to be a stone
the lover would
put it there.

I went upstairs and turned on the
radio and pulled down the
shades.

notice

the swans drown in bilge water,
take down the signs,
test the poisons,
barricade the cow
from the bull,
the peony from the sun,
take the lavender kisses from my night,
put the symphonies out on the streets
like beggars,
get the nails ready,
flog the backs of the saints,
stun frogs and mice for the cat,
burn the enthralling paintings,
piss on the dawn,
my love
is dead.

for Jane

225 days under grass
and you know more than I.

they have long taken your blood,
you are a dry stick in a basket.

is this how it works?

in this room
the hours of love
still make shadows.

when you left
you took almost
everything.

I kneel in the nights
before tigers
that will not let me be.

what you were
will not happen again.

the tigers have found me
and I do not care.

conversation on a telephone

I could tell by the crouch of the cat,
the way it was flattened,
that it was insane with prey;
and when my car came upon it,
it rose in the twilight
and made off
with bird in mouth,
a very large bird, gray,
the wings down like broken love,
the fangs in,
life still there
but not much,
not very much.

the broken love-bird
the cat walks in my mind
and I cannot make him out:
the phone rings,
I answer a voice,
but I see him again and again,
and the loose wings
the loose gray wings,
and this thing held
in a head that knows no mercy;
it is the world, it is ours;
I put the phone down
and the cat-sides of the room
come in upon me
and I would scream,
but they have places for people

who scream;
and the cat walks
the cat walks forever
in my brain.

ants crawl my drunken arms

O ants crawl my drunken arms
and they let Van Gogh sit in a cornfield
and take Life out of the world with a
shotgun,
ants crawl my drunken arms
and they set Rimbaud
to running guns and looking under rocks
for gold,
O ants crawl my drunken arms,
they put Pound in a nuthouse
and made Crane jump into the sea
in his pajamas,
ants, ants crawl my drunken arms
as our schoolboys scream for Willie Mays
instead of Bach,
ants crawl my drunken arms
through the drink I reach
for surfboards and sinks, for sunflowers
and the typewriter falls like a heart-attack
from the table
or a dead Sunday bull,
and the ants crawl into my mouth
and down my throat,
I wash them down with wine
and pull up the shades
and they are on the screen
and on the streets
climbing church towers
and into tire casings
looking for something else
to eat.

a literary discussion

Markov claims I am trying
to stab his soul
but I'd prefer his wife.

I put my feet on the coffee table
and he says,
I don't mind you putting
your feet on the coffee table
except that the legs are wobbly
and the thing
will fall apart
any minute.

I leave my feet on the table
but I'd prefer his wife.

I would rather, says Markov,
entertain a ditch-digger
or a newsvendor
because they are kind enough
to observe the decencies
even though
they don't know
Rimbaud from rat poison.

my empty beercan
rolls to the floor.

that I must die
bothers me less than
a straw, says Markov,

my part of the game
is that I must live
the best I can.

I grab his wife as she walks by,
and then her can is against my belly,
and she has fine knees and breasts
and I kiss her.

it is not so bad, being old, he says,
a calmness sets in, but here's the catch:
to keep calmness and deadness
separate; never to look upon youth
as inferior because you are old,
never to look upon age as wisdom
because you have experience. a
man can be old and a fool—
many are, a man can be young
and wise—few are. a—

for Christ's all sake, I wailed,
shut up!

he walked over and got his cane and
walked out.

you've hurt his feelings, she said,
he thinks you are a great poet.

he's too slick for me, I said,
he's too wise.

I had one of her breasts out.
it was a monstrous
beautiful
thing.

watermelon

and the windows opened that night,
a ceiling dripped the sweat
of a tin god,
and I sat eating a watermelon,
all false red,
water like slow running of rusty
tears,
and I spit out seeds
and swallowed seeds,
and I kept thinking
I am a fool
I am a fool
to eat this watermelon,
but I kept eating
anyhow.

for one I knew

Of all the iron beds in paradise
yours was the most cruel
and I was smoke in your mirror
and you sluiced your hair with jade,
but you were a woman and I was a
boy, but boy enough for an iron bed
and man enough for wine
and you.

now I am a man,
man enough for all,
and you are, you
are
    old

not now so cruel,

now your iron bed
is empty.

when Hugo Wolf went mad—

Hugo Wolf went mad while eating an onion
and writing his 253rd song; it was rainy
April and the worms came out of the ground
humming Tannhäuser, and he spilled his milk
with his ink, and his blood fell out to the walls
and he howled and he roared and he screamed, and
down-
stairs his landlady said, I *knew* it, that rotten son
of a
bitch has dummied up his brain, he's jacked-off
his last piece
of music and now I'll never get the rent, and some-
day he'll be fam-
ous and they'll bury him in the rain, but right now
I wish he'd shut
up that god damned screaming—for my money he's
a silly pansy jackass
and when they move him out of here, I hope they
move in a good solid fish-
erman
or a hangman
or a seller of
Biblical tracts.

riot

the reason for the riot was we kept getting beans
and a guard grabbed a colored boy who threw his on
      the floor
and somebody touched a button
and everybody was grabbing everybody;
I clubbed my best friend behind the ear
somebody threw coffee in my face
(what the hell, you couldn't drink it)
and I got out to the yard
and I heard the guns going
and it seemed like every con had a knife but me,
and all I could do was pray and run
and I didn't have a god and was fat from playing
poker for pennies with my cellmate,
and the warden's voice started coming over the cans,
and I heard later, in the confusion,
the cook raped a sailor,
and I lost my shaving cream, a pack of smokes
and a copy of *The New Yorker*;
also 3 men were shot,
a half dozen knifed,
35 put in the hole,
all yard privileges suspended,
the screws as jittery as L.A. bookies,
the prison radio off,
real quiet,
visitors sent home,
but the next morning
we did get our mail—
a letter from St. Louis:

Dear Charles, I am sorry you are in prison,
but you cannot break the law,
and there was a pressed carnation,
perfume, the looming of outside,
kisses and panties,
laughter and beer,
and that night for dinner
they marched us all back down
to the beans.

meanwhile

neither does this mean
the dead are
at the door
begging bread
before
the stockpiles
blow
like all the
storms and hell
in one big love,
but anyhow
I rented a 6 dollar a week
room
in Chinatown
with a window as large as the
side of the world
filled with night flies and neon,
lighted like Broadway
to frighten away rats,
and I walked into a bar and sat down,
and the Chinaman looked at my rags
and said
no credit
and I pulled out a hundred dollar bill
and asked for a cup of Confucius juice
and 2 China dolls with slits of eyes
just about the size of the rest of them
slid closer
and we sat
and we
waited.

a poem is a city

a poem is a city filled with streets and sewers
filled with saints, heroes, beggars, madmen,
filled with banality and booze,
filled with rain and thunder and periods of
drought, a poem is a city at war,
a poem is a city asking a clock why,
a poem is a city burning,
a poem is a city under guns
its barbershops filled with cynical drunks,
a poem is a city where God rides naked
through the streets like Lady Godiva,
where dogs bark at night, and chase away
the flag; a poem is a city of poets,
most of them quite similar
and envious and bitter . . .
a poem is this city now,
50 miles from nowhere,
9:09 in the morning,
the taste of liquor and cigarettes,
no police, no lovers, walking the streets,
this poem, this city, closing its doors,
barricaded, almost empty,
mournful without tears, aging without pity,
the hardrock mountains,
the ocean like a lavender flame,
a moon destitute of greatness,
a small music from broken windows . . .

a poem is a city, a poem is a nation,
a poem is the world . . .

and now I stick this under glass
for the mad editor's scrutiny,
and night is elsewhere
and faint gray ladies stand in line,
dog follows dog to estuary,
the trumpets bring on gallows
as small men rant at things
they cannot do.

the cat

the hunter goes by my window
4 feet locked in the bright stillness of a
yellow and blue
night.

cruel strangeness takes hold in wars, in
gardens—
the yellow and blue night explodes before
me, atomic, surgical,
full of starlit
devils . . .

then the cat leaps up on the
fence, a tubby dismay,
stupid, lonely,
whiskers like an old lady in the
supermarket
and naked as the
moon.

I am temporarily
delighted.

hermit in the city

Idle in the forest of my room
with tungsten trees, owl boiling coffee,
webs cowled in gold over windows
staring outward into hell;
cigarette breath: statues of perfection,
not stuffed or whirled in cancers
of ranting;
engines and wheels crawl to gaseous
ends along the sabre-tooth;
my trees climb with monkey-rhyme,
climb out through the ceiling
breaking TV antennas and
the dull howl of canned laughter,
canned humor, canned death;
idle, idle in this forest,
calla lilies, grass, stone,
all nighttime level peace
of no bombers or faces,
and I dream the stone dream,
the grass dream,
the river running through my
fingerbones
one hundred and fifty years away,
leaving shots of grit and gold
and radium,
lifted and turned
by dizzied fish
and dropped,
raising flecks of sand
in my sleep . . .

The owl spits his coffee,
my monkeys chit the gibberish plan,
and my walls,
my walls help endure the seizing.

II

*I dreamed I drank an Arrow shirt
and stole a broken
pail*

all-yellow flowers

through the venetian blinds I saw a fat man in a brown coat
(with a head I can only describe as like a marshmallow)
drag the casket from the hearse: it was battleship gray
with all-yellow flowers.
they put it on a roller that was hidden in purple drape
and the marshmallow-man and one pin-crisp bloodless woman
walked for *him* up the incline . . . and!—
gore-bell-horror-sheer-sheen-world-ending-moment!—
almost losing IT there, once—
I could see the body rolling out
like one loose dice in a losing game—the arms waving
windmills and legs kicking autumn footballs.

they made it into the church
and I remained outside
opening my brain to living sunlight.

in the room with me she was singing and rolling her
long golden hair. (this is true Arturo, and that is what
makes it so simple.)
"I just saw them take in a body,"
I fashioned to her.

it's autumn, it's trees, it's telephone wires,
and she sings some song I can't understand, some High Mass
of Life.

she went on singing but I wanted to die
I wanted yellow flowers like her golden hair
I wanted yellow-singing and the sun.

this is true, and that is what makes it so strange:
I wanted to be opened and untangled, and
tossed away.

what seems to be the trouble, gentlemen?

the service was bad
and the bellboy kept bringing in towels
at the wrong moment.
drunk, I finally clubbed him along
the side of the head.
he was a little man and he fell
like an October leaf,
quite done,
and when the fuzz came up
I had the sofa in front of the door
and the chain on,
the 2nd movement of Brahms' First Symphony
and had my hand halfway up the ass
of a broad old enough to be my grandmother
and they broke the god damned door,
pushed the sofa aside;
I slapped the screaming chippy
and turned and asked,
what seems to be the trouble, gentlemen?
and some young kid who had never shaved
brought his stick down against my head
and in the morning I was in the prison ward
chained to my bed
and it was hot,
the sweat coming down through the white
senseless sheet,
and they asked all sorts of silly questions
and I knew I'd be late for work,
which worried me immensely.

spring swan

swans die in the Spring too
and there it floated
dead on a Sunday
sideways
circling in current
and I walked to the rotunda
and overhead
gods in chariots
dogs, women
circled,
and death
ran down my throat
like a mouse,
and I heard the people coming
with their picnic bags
and laughter,
and I felt guilty
for the swan
as if death
were a thing of shame
and like a fool
I walked away
and left them
my beautiful swan.

remains

things are good as I am not dead yet
and the rats move in the beercans,
the papersacks shuffle like small dogs,
and her photographs are stuck onto a painting
by a dead German and she too is dead
and it took 14 years to know her
and if they give me another 14
I will know her yet . . .
her photos stuck over the glass
neither move nor speak,
but I even have her voice on tape,
and she speaks some evenings,
her again
so real she laughs
says the thousand things,
the one thing I always ignored;
this will never leave me:
that I had love
and love died;
a photo and a piece of tape
is not much, I have learned late,
but give me 14 days or 14 years,
I will kill any man
who would touch or take
whatever's left.

the moment of truth

he died a suicide in a Detroit hotel room
on skid row
and he was stiff when they found him,
rat poison . . .
I was managing the place then,
trying to collect rents and
emptying the trash,
and I stood there and watched them put the needle in him,
his eyes were wide open and one of them slid his eyes
shut, and then the needle began to take hold,
he had died stiff upright in the chair
and he began to loosen up
and they found a couple of letters from his sister
in another city, threw him on the stretcher and took him
down the stairs. the sheets were still kinda clean
so I just made the bed over again, cleaned out the dresser,
and when I walked out, all the winos were in the hall
in their pants and dirty undershirts, needing shaves and
        something to
drink, and I told them: "all right, all you monkeys
clear the god damned halls! you hurt my eyesight!"
"a man died, sir. he was our friend," one of them said.
it was Benny the Dip. "all right, Benny," I told him,
"you've got one night left in here to get up the rent!"
you should have seen the rest of them disappear:
death doesn't matter a damn when you need a place
        to sleep.

on the fire suicides of the buddhists

"They only burn themselves to reach Paradise."
                                    —Mme. Nhu

original courage is good,
motivation be damned,
and if you say they are trained
to feel no pain,
are they
guaranteed this?
is it still not *possible*
to die for somebody else?

you sophisticates
who lay back and
make statements of explanation,
I have seen the red rose burning
and this means more.

a division

I live in an old house where nothing
screams victory
reads history
where nothing
plants flowers

sometimes my clock falls
sometimes my sun is like a tank on fire

I do not ask
your armies
or
your kisses
or
your death
I have my
own

my hands have arms
my arms have shoulders
my shoulders have me
I have me
you have me when you can see me
but I don't like you
to see me

I do not like you to see that
I have eyes in my head
and can walk
and
I do not want to

answer your questions
I do not want to
amuse you
I do not want you to
amuse me
or sicken me
or talk about
anything

I do not want to
love you

I do not want to
save you

I do not want your arms
I do not want your
shoulders

I have me
you have you

let that
be.

conversation with a lady sipping a straight shot

and Joe he was not much good
even at half past 40, he insensibly
loved whore and horse like the average man,
his age would love what brought up color
out of the stem of a dahlia, but so it goes,
the gods break us in half with more than
lightning, twice married twice divorced,
who can ask for more than bloodshot eyes
and bumblebeebelly, good men are broken
daily in the Korea of useless sunlight;
quitting jobs, getting fired more than rockets,
knowing nothing, absolutely nothing
except maybe the way he wanted his haircut,
bouncing like a 16-year-old kid out of a
bad dream, always late for work
but never late for the first race
or the end stool down at the HAPPY NIGHT.
the saying is, Joe never grew up
but in another way he never grew down either,
trying to puff life into himself through his
cheap cigar and flat jukebox music,
or fat June who didn't care either,
telling her over and over,
Baby, wait'll you see what I've got!
as if the whole thing were something new
and fat June staring into her all-important beer
shaking it and enjoying it
as she would never enjoy herself again.

and when Joe went, a child went,
but they remember him: the whores, the bartenders,

the bosses, the state unemployment offices,
and the jocks—
the way he used to stand down by the rail
and say as they paraded past:
"Hi, Willie! How's your mother today?"
or, "Eddie, you oughta get one made of wood,
the way you're riding lately."

Joe I saw on that last night and he threw his
glass into the mirror and the bartender
mad as hell chased him with a baseball bat
swinging at his balls and everything else,
driving him out into the street and into the path
of a bull with one horn that didn't sound,
a new Cad a lot tougher than Joe and a lot more
valuable, and that's the way the scales balance:
broken mirror, broken Joe.

and when I went in the next night the mirror was
still broken and Helen, fat Helen, was shaking her beer,
and I bought her a shot and I said, "Baby, I've got
something to show you, something like you've never
seen before."

and she smiled, but it wasn't what she was thinking.

the way it will happen inside a can of peaches

to die with your boots on
while writing poetry
is not as glorious
as riding a horse
down Broadway
with a stick of dynamite
in your teeth,
but neither is
adding the sum total
of all the planets
named or visible
to man,
and the horse was a gray,
the man's name was
Sanchez or Kandinsky,
it was 79 degrees
and the children kept
yelling,
hog hog
we are tired
blow us to hell.

scene in a tent outside the cotton fields
of Bakersfield:

we fought for 17 days inside that tent
thrusting and counter-thrusting
but finally she got away
and I walked outside
and spit
in the dirty sand.

Abdullah, I said, why don't you
wash your shorts? you've been
wearing the same
shorts
for 17 years.

Effendi, he said, it's the sun,
the sun cleans everything. what
went with the girl?

I don't know if I couldn't
please her
or if I couldn't
catch her. she was
pretty young.

what did she cost, Effendi?

17 camel.

he whistled through his broken
teeth. aren't you going
to catch her?

howinthehell how? can I get
my camels back?

you are an American, he said.

I walked into the tent
fell upon the ground
and held my head
within
my hands.

suddenly she burst within
the tent
laughing madly,
Americano,
        Americano!

please
        go away
I said quietly.

men are, she said sitting down and rolling down
her stockings, some parts titty and some parts
tiger. you don't mind
if I roll down
my stockings?

I don't mind, I said,
if you roll down the top
of your dress. whores are
always rolling down
their hose. please
go away. I read where
the cruiser crew passed the helmet
for the red cross; I think I'll

have them pass it
to brace your flabby
butt.

have 'em pass the helmet twice, dad,
she said, howcum you don't love me
no more?

I been thinking, I said,
how can Love have a urinary tract
and distended bowels?
pack up, daughter, and flow,
maneuver out of the mansions
of my sight!

you forget, daddy-o, we're in
my tent!

oh, christ, I said, the trivialities
of private ownership! where's my
hat?

you were wearing a towel, dad, but
kiss me, daddy, hold me in your arms!

I walked over and mauled her breasts.

I drink too much beer, she said,
I can't help it if I
piss.

we fucked for 17 days.

night animal

I have never seen such an animal
except perhaps once,
but that is another story—
there it stood,
no lion
yet no dog
no deer yet deer
frozen nose
and eye, all eye gathering all the
moonlight that hung in trees;
and everywhere the people slept;
I saw bombers over Brazil,
cathedrals choked in silk,
the gray dice of Vegas,
a Van Gogh over the kitchen sink.

home, I poured a drink
took off my gloves   you god damned thing
why could you have not been a woman
with all your beauty,
with all your beauty
I have not found her yet.

on the train to Del Mar

I get on the train on the way to the track
it's down near Dago
and this gives some space and rolling and
I have my pint
and I walk to the barcar for a couple of
beers
and I weave upon the floor—
THACK THACK THACKA THACK THACK
    THACKA THACK—
and some of it comes back
a little of it comes back
like some green in a leaf after a long
dryness

and the sun crashes into the barcar like a
bull and the bartender sees that
I am feeling good
he smiles a real smile and
asks—
    "How's it going?"

how's it going? my heels are down
my shoes cracked
I am wearing my father's pants and he died
10 years ago
I need 8 teeth pulled
my intestine has a partial blockage
I puff on a dime cigar

    "Great!" I answer him,
    "how you making?"

glory glory glory and the train rolls on
past the sea
past the sand and
down in between the
cliffs.

I thought of ships, of armies, hanging on . . .

I have practiced death for so long
and still I have not learned it,
and tonight I came in
and my goldfish was not in his bowl,
he had leaped
for reasons of his own
(I had changed the water; it might have been
a fly . . .)
and he was now on the rug
with black spots upon his golden body,
and he was still and he was stiff
but I put him back in the water
(some sound told me to do this)
and I seemed to see the gills move,
a large air bubble formed
but the body was still stiff
but miraculously
it did not float flat—
the tail part was down in the water,
and I thought of ships, of armies,
hanging on,
and then I saw the small fins
near the underside of the head
move
and I sat down on the couch
and tried to read,
tried not to think
that the woman who had given me these fish
was now dead 6 months,
the world going on past living things
now no longer living,

and the other fish had died.
he had overeaten, he had eaten his meal
and most of the meal of the small one,
and now the woman was gone
and the small one was stiff,
and an hour later
when I got up
he floated flat and finished;
his eyes looking up at me did not look at me
but into places I could not see,
and the slave carried the master,
this goldfish with black spots
and dumped him into the toilet
and flushed him away.

I put the bowl in the corner
and thought, I really cannot stand
much more of this.

dead fish, dead ladies, dead wars.

it does seem a miracle to see anybody alive
and now somebody on the radio is playing
a guitar very slowly and I think, yes,
he too: his fingers, his hands, his mind,
and his music goes on but it is very still
it is very quiet, and I am tired.

war and piece

all the efforts of the Spanish to effect peace
were in vain and Domenico came over the hill
and shot the white chicken and raped the woman
in the hut, and then he rode up the road
noticing the pink anemones, the lazy toads,
and when he got to town he ate a hot tamale,
and through the window he saw the fleet
and the fleet put its guns even with the town,
he saw that, and in came a wind of fire,
and in the smoke he grabbed the cigarette girl
and raped her, then he got back on his mule
which stepped carefully over the dead
and he rode back to the village where his own hut
still stood, and the old lady was outside
rubbing clothes on rocks by the stream,
and in the air came the planes
looking them over
banking their wings
and finally deciding
that they were not worth the bombs,
they left
like large undecided butterflies,
and Domenico went inside and fell
upon the floor
and the old lady came in
wiggling what was left,
and he said, *war is a horrible thing,*
and he wondered if anybody would ever bother
     to rape her,
he would not stop them, they

could have it, not much there, nothing,
and he decided that sleep was better than nothing
and he went to sleep.

18 cars full of men thinking of what could have been

driving in from the track
I saw a woman in green
all rump and breast and dizziness running
across the street.
she was as sexy as a
green and drunken antelope and
when she got to the curbing she
tripped and fell
down and
sat in the gutter and
I sat there in my car
looking at her and
oddly
I felt most impassive as if
nothing had happened and
I sat there looking at this
green creature until
a moving van 60 feet long came
to a stop and
helped the
lady
up.
a young man in white overalls
flushed red and the girl was built
all around all around and
stupid with falling and stupid with life and
swaying on the tower stilts of her
heels
she stood there rubbing her
white knees and

the young man kept talking to
her
he was big dumb blond pink and lonely
but then
the woman asked him
where the nearest bar was and
he grinned and pointed down the street and
gave it
up
he got back into the truck and
60 feet full of
furniture and blanket and stove
pulled on down the street
and the green antelope
crossed the street
toward the bar
wobbling and shaking
shaking and wobbling
everything and
we sat transfixed and
watching
until
in the backed-up traffic
behind me
a man of strength
honked
and I put the thing in drive
slowing for the big dip
by the market
that could tear your car in
half
and they all followed me
slowing for the dip
too:
18 cars full of men thinking of
what could have been—

about the one who
got away and
it was about sunset and
heavy traffic and heavy
life.

the screw-game

one of the terrible things is
really
being in bed
night after night
with a woman you no longer
want to screw.

they get old, they don't look very good
anymore—they even tend to
snore, lose
spirit.

so, in bed, you turn sometimes,
your foot touches hers—
god, *awful!*—
and the night is out there
beyond the curtains
sealing you together
in the
tomb.

and in the morning you go to the
bathroom, pass in the hall, talk,
say odd things; eggs fry, motors
start.

but sitting across
you have 2 strangers
jamming toast into mouths
burning the sullen head and gut with
coffee.

in 10 million places in America
it is the same—
stale lives propped against each
other
and no place to
go.

you get in the car
and you drive to work
and there are more strangers there, most of them
wives and husbands of somebody
else, and besides the guillotine of work, they
flirt and joke and pinch, sometimes tend to
work off a quick screw somewhere—
they can't do it at home—
and then
the drive back home
waiting for Christmas or Labor Day or
Sunday or
something.

a night of Mozart

They slit his pockets and shot him in his car,
eighteen hundred dollars split four ways,
and I used to see him at the track
watching the tote
and going the last-flick bullrush toward the window;
he never took a drink
and he never took a woman home with him,
and he never spoke to anyone,
and I never spoke to anyone either
except to order a drink
or if a hustler had good legs and ass
to let her know
over a scotch and water
that later would be o.k.;
what I am getting at is
that this guy was a pro,
it was a business with him,
he didn't come out to holler and get drunk
and get fucked—
he came out to *make it,* which is better
than punching another man's timeclock;
when I saw him bullrushing the $50 window
late in the year
I knew he was making it much better than I;
the board had showed a lot of false flashes,
some nut with a roll was dropping in one or two grand
at the last minute, but this guy was just that,
a nut with money, and we finally had to go through
the routine of finding out what he was betting
and flushing the horse out
before we got our bets down; this made one sweaty

late bullrush . . . anyhow, the quiet one didn't
worry about this and always laid his bet a little ahead
of time and walked off; he kept getting better,
his clothes looked better, he looked calmer,
and you could see him off to the side,
after most races, shoving bills into his wallet,
and Jeanette, one of the better hustlers, said,
"I'd start him off with a blow-job and then twist
his nuts until he told me how he did it . . ."
"Would you do that to me, baby?" I asked.
"With your method of play you're lucky to have
admission," she said downing a drink that had cost me
85¢. "Do you still have a collection of Mozart?"
I asked her. "What's that got to do with it?" she asked.
I walked off.

I read about it in the papers next day. Witnesses
said there were 3 of them and a woman at the wheel.
I saw Jeanette at the bar. "Hello, Mozart," she said.
She looked a little nervous and at the same time she
seemed to feel pretty good. "I'll take a double
shot right now," I said. "And after the next race,
I think I'll have a vodka. I'm going to mix them all day.
        Haven't
been real drunk in a couple of years."

She watched me lighting a cigarette, then I told her, "Also, I
want a pack of smokes, and you are going home with me
        tonight and
we are going to listen to Mozart all night. You are going to
like it. You are going to have to like it."

She paid for the drink. "You're looking for trouble," she told
me. "Bitch," I said, "I have been trying to commit suicide
        for
years."

I had a good day. We went home and listened to Mozart for
  hours.
She was as good as ever on the springs. Only this time there
  was
no charge. Then she cried half the night and said she loved
  me.
I knew what that was for.

The next afternoon at the track I didn't speak to her, and
  I won
one hundred and twelve dollars, not counting drinks and
  admission,
and I kept looking back through the rearview window as
  I drove,
bigtime, and then I began to laugh, shit, they knew I was
  nothing,
I was safe; I should tell the screws but when a man is dead
the screws can't bring him back.

I got home and opened a fifth of scotch, tired of Mozart
I tried *The Rake's Progress* by Strav.
I read the Racing Form for about 30 minutes, put in a long
  distance
call to some woman in Sacramento, drank a little more and
  went to
bed, alone, about 11:30.

sleeping woman

I sit up in bed at night and listen to you
snore
I met you in a bus station
and now I wonder at your back
sick white and stained with
children's freckles
as the lamp divests the unsolvable
sorrow of the world
upon your sleep.

I cannot see your feet
but I must guess that they are
most charming feet.

who do you belong to?
are you real?
I think of flowers, animals, birds
they all seem more than good
and so clearly
real.

yet you cannot help being a
woman. we are each selected to be
something. the spider, the cook.
the elephant. it is as if we were each
a painting and hung on some
gallery wall.

—and now the painting turns
upon its back, and over a curving elbow
I can see ½ a mouth, one eye and

almost a nose.
the rest of you is hidden
out of sight
but I know that you are a
contemporary, a modern living
work
perhaps not immortal
but we have
loved.

please continue to
snore.

when you wait for the dawn to crawl through the
screen like a burglar to take your life away—

the snake had crawled the hole,
and she said,
tell me about
yourself.

and
I said,
I was beaten down
long ago
in some alley
in another
world.

and she said,
we're all
like pigs
slapped down some lane,
our
grassbrains
singing
toward the
blade.

by
god,
you're an
odd one,
I said.

we
sat there
smoking
cigarettes
at
5
in the morning.

poem while looking at an encyclopedia:

it is a page of reptiles, green pink fuchsia
slime motif
sexual organs
lips teeth fangs
in the grass of my brain
bringing down 1917 Spads,
games with toy cars
in a boy's backyard;
and eggs eggs eggs
of the hognose snake
she circles them in the sun,
life is an electric whip,
and ha!—the copperhead
he looks about, tiny brain
in the air searching
a wiseness as small as
seething to stroke a death;
and the horned toad:
fat little shitter in
fake armour
he blinks blinks
blinks in the sun
watching the flies
he is a tired old man
beyond hardly caring—
he just looks and waits
very dry
(wanting storm)
powerless
(without desire for)
ungifted he

waits to be eaten;
and the gila monster
and the collared lizard,
the box turtle,
the chuckwalla,
here they go along the page,
and through rock and cacti
I suppose they are beautiful
in their slow horror,
and at the bottom
an alligator puts his eye upon me
and we look
he and I; he breathes and hungers
on a flat dream, and so
this is the way we will be spread
across the page,—
teeth, title, poesy,
alligator heart,
as the sky falls down.

3 lovers

I saw them
sitting in the lamplight and
I went in
and
he talked
waving his hands
jesus
his face was red
and
he talked
he wanted to be
right
he waved his hands
but when I left
he just sat there
and
she sat there
in the chair across from him
and
I got into my car
and backed out the drive
and
left them there
to do
whatever
they wanted to
do.

did I ever tell you?

Did I ever tell you
about the damn fool who
liked to make love
in front of a
        picture window?

And there was the one
who took the phonograph back,
and the one who
broke the lampshades
and the one with the
little golden hairs on his
        chest.

And the one
on the kitchen floor,
and the one who
hunted for the mouth
of the Orinoco River.

And the tall one who
became a forest ranger
and left a note with Roger
confessing he was queer
        (but Roger already knew).

Then there's the communist—he's in
Canada
or Florida, only I think
he's somebody else under this other
name, and I have a photo of him

crawling out of a rowboat;
he has lovely gray hair and his face
is sort of blue
and he writes these
    long love letters.

And Edward was a queer—but so very gentle;
he lit candles, had a sense of humor and
very hairy legs—like one of those land
crabs
    or a coconut.

And Jerry was just like a horse—
if I looked him in the eye
he couldn't
kiss me.
(He just pretended he was gay
but he wasn't.)
(I can tell. Oh, I can always tell.)

Then there was my desert
romance—I really don't like to tell
about it, but since you *asked*—
I think he really
loved me.
I got drunk and
fell off my horse
and broke my
arm
when we tried to jump a fence
riding double-saddle
and his wife threatened to
kill me
    so
        I
            left town.

I used to go up on the
roof with Manny.
He was strange.
Parents spoiled him.
We looked at the moon through
a telescope: I stood
at the big end
and held it up
and he sat down
at the little end
and looked through it.

And Carl has my *Drama*
Through the Ages, from
Euripides to Miller.
(I must write him for it. You
won't mind?) That Carl—

it was my birthday
and I came in
and he was out
cold drunk
on the sofa
and I threw
some flowers at him
(vase and all)
and he stood up
and showed me the tiniest
gold bracelet
in a little felt box,
and I cried.
(Oh yes, I loved him. I really
loved him—he was so kind,
and he was always writing mother—

"Where's Rita at, please tell me!"
but mother
      never told him.)

Then there was that old bastard German
they never know when to give it up.
He was bald and I hated him,
he looked like a sick frog
and his breath was bad,
but the funniest thing
was all this hair on
his belly. I could never
figure it.
He had plenty of money
but he was married,
the old bastard,
and he told me
he loved me,
and he hired me as a
secretary,
he was always playing around,
the old bastard,
and I finally ran away,
though I *could* have taken him
from his wife
but I couldn't stand the old
bastard.

Vincent?
No. He was nothing. He was frightened
of his brother.
"My brother!" he'd scream
and we'd all run out the back door
and into the garage naked
or just in panties and bras.
I made curtains for his house

and he called me daughter
and I cooked for him
and he wrote everything in a little
black book and wore a sailing cap.
He dropped money on the floor
and played the organ . . .
wrote an opera for Organ
called the *Emperor of San Francisco*.
But I liked him mainly because
he knew the kids,
drove me to Newman once to meet them,
and once, before he got real tight
he sent me money
when I was stranded in the islands.

And Gus—he was just like a father to me—
I knew him so long.
I met him in the islands
when I was stranded.
I think he saved my life.
I got fired for being caught in the
barracks.
But he understood.
Oh, I know you don't like him,
but he's so *understanding*.
And when Vincent sent the money
we both came stateside.
He said he wanted to marry me
but he had to take care of his
mother
who had some kind of
lifelong disease.
He's always running back to
those islands,
so completely lost,
utterly lost.

You'd hardly know him now.
He's stopped drinking
and weighs 297,
(and he kissed just like you,
and had little wires in his left
leg, but he'd never tell me . . .)

. . . and the chauffeur
walked into the room
with a basket
with a live chicken
in it. This guy grabbed the chicken
around the neck
and whirled it
around and around
and you should have heard
that chicken scream
and then he cut it with a knife
and the blood
flew like rain
and this guy
played his piccolo
and watched my eyes,
and that's all that happened,
even though he had made me
take off my dress.
He gave me $25
but somehow
the whole thing
made me sick.

Nicholas was a queer
and impotent,
and he was my lover.
He still has my
e.e. cummings.

The first one was insane.
He blew
through fig leaves
while sitting on the coffee table
his hands tangled in my hair.
He played the oboe
and you know what
they say about the oboe:
they took him away
from me
and he was like a child.
I gave the oboe to a ballet dancer
who broke his
leg on
a camp stool
while
hiking
in the Adirondacks.

I was engaged to Arlington
only three weeks.
And he tore the ring from my finger
claiming he didn't
want to marry the whole
queer army.
Later he cried on my shoulder
and told me he was a queen bee
and a general
and that he had been kidding himself
all his life.
I cried when he left.

Ralph was the only one, I think,
who ever loved me,
but he didn't appreciate the finer
things:

he thought that Van Gogh used to pitch for
Brooklyn and that George Sand played
opposite Zsa Zsa Gabor.
And when he sent money from East Lansing
I bought a hi-fi set and a toy bull
with blue eyes
and called him Keithy-pot.
I sent Ralph a pressed azalea and a photo
of me
bending over
in a bikini.

Sherman was afraid of the dark.
He died swallowing a
cherry seed. Roger—I've told
you
about him; Roger started
a good story once
but he never finished it.
      It was about a queer
sitting at a table
at a night club
and these people came up—
but, oh, I can't explain it.

Peter will kill himself some day.
Art will kill himself.
Tommy set fire to the bed and
beat his mother. I only
lived with him
because of her. We went
to Alkaseltzer Mass
together. Once he
hit her when she
got off the streetcar.

Then he hit me. I hated him,
but she was like a mother to me.
And then I met you.

Remember that Sunday at
the Round Duck?
You said,
      let's go to
        Mexico.
And you took me up
to your place
and read Erle Stanley Gardner
and then you hung out
the window.
You looked like my father.
You should have known my father.
He was a drunkard.

Oh, I'm so glad I met you.
You make me
feel so
good. Darling *you* are a
man.
The only real
MAN
I've *ever* known!
Oh dear, how I've
waited!
My hands are cold and
you have the *funniest*
feet!

I love you . . .

song of my typewriter:

the best way to think is not at all—
my banjo screams in the brush
like a trapped rabbit (do rabbits
scream? never mind: this is an
alcoholic dream);
machine guns, I say,
the altarboys,
the wet nurses,
the fat newsboys,
rubber-lipped delegates
of the precious life;
my banjo screams
sing
sing through the darkened dream,
green grow green,
take gut:
death, at last,
is no headache.

and the moon and the stars and the world:

long walks at
night—
that's what's good
for the
soul:
peeking into windows
watching tired
housewives
trying to fight
off
their beer-maddened
husbands.

the sharks

the sharks knock on my door
and enter and ask favors;
how they puff in my chairs
looking about the room,
and they ask for deeds:
light, air, money,
anything they can get—
beer, cigarettes, half dollars, dollars,
fives, dimes,
all this as if my survival were assured,
as if my time were nothing
and their presence valuable.

well, we all have our sharks, I'm sure,
and there's only one way to get them off
before they hack and nibble you to death—
stop feeding them; they will find
other bait; you fattened them
the last dozen times around—
now set them out
to sea.

fag, fag, fag

he wrote,
you are a humorless ass,
I was only pulling your leg about D.
joining the Foreign Legion, and
D. is about as much fag as
Winston Churchill.

hmm, I thought, I am in contact with the
greatest minds of my
generation. clever! Winnie is dead so he
can't be a
fag.

the letter continued,
you guys in California are fag-happy,
all you do is sit around and think about
fags. just the same I will send you the anti-war
materials I and others wrote, although I
doubt it will stop the
war.

10 years ago he had sent me a photo of
D. and himself at a picnic ground.
D. was dressed in a Foreign Legion uniform,
there was a bottle of wine,
and a table with one tableleg
crooked.

I thought it over for 10 years and then
answered:

I have nothing against 2 men sleeping together
so long as I am not one of those 2
men.

I didn't infer which one was the
fag.

anyway, today I got the anti-war materials
in the mail, but he's right:
it won't stop the war or anything
else.

Ivan the Terrible

found it difficult
either to stand or
to bend over

was fat with
big eyes and
low
forehead
had a perennial
smile
due to an
underslung
jaw

killed his eldest son
with blows
in a moment
of anger

appeared to be uncomfortable
after the age
of
40

excelled in progress
and
butchery

died in 1584
at the age of

54, weighing
209
pounds

last summer
they removed his
skeleton
from the Arkhangelsk Church
in the Kremlin
to make a
lifelike
bust

now
he's almost done
and looks like
a 20th century
bus driver

the bones of my uncle

(for J.B. who never read the stuff)

the bones of my uncle
rode a motorcycle in Arcadia
and raped a housewife
within a garage
hung with rakes and hoses
the bones of my Uncle
left behind
1: a jar of peanut butter
and
2: two girls named
Katherine &
Betsy and
3: a ragged wife who cried
continually.
the bones of my Uncle
played horses
too
and
made counterfeit money—
mostly dimes, and the F.B.I. wanted him for
something more serious
although what it was
I have since
forgotten.
the bones of my Uncle
stretched the long way
seemed too short
and looked at

coming toward you
bent like bows
beneath the knees.

the bones of my Uncle
smoked and cussed
and they were buried
where bones are buried
who have no
money.

I almost forgot to tell you:
his bones were named "John"
and
had green eyes
which did not
last.

a last shot on two good horses

it was about 10 years ago at Hollywood Park—
I had a shackjob, 2 cars, a house, a dog as big as Nero
      drunk,
and I was making it with the horses, or I thought I was,
but going into the 7th race I was down to my last $50
and I put the $50 on Determine and then I wanted a cup
      of coffee
but I only had a dime left and coffee was then 15¢.

I went into the crapper and I wanted to flush myself away,
they had me, all I had left was that piece of paper in my
      wallet,
and I would have been willing to sell that back for $40
but I was ashamed. well, I went out and watched the race
and Determine won.

I collected and set aside a ten and put the remainder all on
My Boy Bobby. My Boy Bobby made it. I collected and
      stood over in
a corner, separating the 50s and the 20s and tens and fives,
and then I drove on in, I gave her the thumb up as I drove
      up the drive,
and when I got inside I threw all the money up into the air.

She was a beautiful whore and her eyes almost came out
      when she saw
that, and the dog ran in and snatched a ten and ran into the
      kitchen,
and I was pouring drinks and she said, "hey, the hound got
      a tenner!"
and I said, "hell, let him have it!" we drank 'em down.

then I said, "umm, I think I'll get that ten anyhow," and I
    walked in
and took it from him, it was only chewed a little, and that
    night
on the bed she showed me all the tricks in wonderland, and
    later
it rained and we listened to Carmen and drank and laughed
    all night long.

days and nights like that just don't happen too often.

III

& the great white horses come up
& lick the frost of the dream

no grounding in the classics

I haven't slept
for 3 nights
or 3 days
and my eyes are more
red than white;
I laugh in the
mirror,
and I have been
listening to the clock
tick
and the gas
of my heater
smells
a hot thick
heavy
smell, run
through with the sounds
of cars,
cars strung up
like ornaments
in my head, but
I have read
the classics
and on my couch
sleeps a wine-soaked
whore
who for the first
time
has heard
Beethoven's 9th,

and bored,
has fallen asleep,
politely
listening.

just think, daddy, she said,
with your brains
you might be the first man
to copulate
on the moon.

drawing of a band concert on a matchbox

life on paper is so much more
pleasurable:
there are no bombs or flies or
landlords or starving
cats,
and I am in the kitchen
staring down at the blue lake of the
concertmaster
and also the trees
rowboats, boy with American flag
lady in yellow with fan
Civil War veteran
girl with balloon
spotted dog
sailboat,
the peace of an ancient day
with the sun dreaming old
battles—
John L. Sullivan emptying the pint
in his dressing room
and getting ready to whip the world like a
bad child—
far from our modern life
where a doctor sticks something in your side,
saying, "is something making you nervous? something is
killing you."

I open the matchbox, take out a beautiful wooden match
and light a cigar.

I look out the window. it is raining. there will be nothing
in the park today except bums and madmen.
I blow the smoke against the wet glass and wonder what I
        am doing
inside here
dry and dying and
I hear the rain as a toilet flushes through the wall
(a living neighbor)
and the flowers open their arms for love.

I sit down next to the lady in yellow with the fan and
she smiles at me
and we talk we talk
only I can't hear for all the music
"your name? your name?" I keep asking
but she only smiles at me
and the dog is howling.

but yellow is my favorite color
(Van Gogh liked it too)
yellow
and I do not blow smoke in her face
and I am there
I am actually down there in the matchbox
and I am here too.

she smiles
and I lay her right on the
stove
and it is
hot
hot
the American flag waves in
battle—
play your music concertmaster

in your red coat
with your hot July buttocks.

the balloon pops and I walk across a kitchen
on a rainy day in February
to check on eggs and bread and
wine and sanity

to check on glue
to paste nice pictures
on these walls.

bad night

I am fairly drunk and there is a man jumping
up and down on the floor in his shack next door
he's rough on the floorboards and I listen to his
dance while my wife is in the can and Fidelio is on
our radio, and today at the track I lost $70 and a woman
got her foot caught in the escalator, and the drunks
hollered at the usher: REVERSE IT! THROW IT IN
REVERSE! meanwhile, the red blood and the gamblers
        and
myself watching the tote for a meaningful flash and I
        dumped it in
the wrong place.
now the man has stopped jumping on the floor and
has opened his bible. well, it has been a bad
summer for all of us. a particular feeling
a flailing feeling of too much. we are shocked
almost senseless with the demand to put on our
socks, we hang like paintings of blue-skinned
virgins before young boys in dementia, & it's
too much hair on the neck and flowers dying in a
bowl. my wife comes out of the
can.
    are you all right? she
  asks. yeah, I
say.

down by the wings

they speak of angels or she
speaks of angels
from a plateglass window overlooking the
Sunset Strip
(she has these visions)
(I don't have these visions)
but maybe angels prefer people with
money
daughters of rich farmers who are dying of
throat cancer in Brazil.
myself—I keep seeing these
wingless creatures of mean story and dismal
intent
and she says
when I defame her
dream:

      you are trying to
      pull me down
      by the wings.

she's going to Europe in the summer—
Greece, Italy, most probably
Paris and she's
taking some of her angels with
her.
not all
but some.
now there's this half-Chinese boy who used to
sleep on fire escapes
the Negro homosexual who plays chess and
recited Shelley at the Sensualist

then there's the one who has real talent with the
brush (Nickey) but who simply can't get
started
somehow and
there's also Sieberling who cries because he
loves his mother (actually).

many of these
angels
will leave town and
flow around the
Arch of Triumph
to be photographed or
to chase beetles at
9 rue Git-le-Coeur, and
it's going to be a hot and
lonesome summer
for many of us when
the devil walks in and retakes Hollywood
once more.

fire

schoolgirls in tight skirts and first heels
came

sparrows flew away and fat landlords parted from their
electric mirrors

skinny housewives with runny noses and dirty aprons
came

and the fire engine: polished wailing disorder spilling
intestines of water
came

firemen in helmets
firemen with axes
came

god, a tree 90 feet high
BURNING
A HOUSE BURNING RED
   tolling
       lordward
the grass melting and yelling on the top of the
ground and
those smokesweet pictures of bluegray putting the
      whole sky out of
place

and all the while nobody saying anything just
watching
what the flames did

like something busted out
finally and having its
say

we all came
together.

one for the old man

standing in the plaza I can hear speeches about a new
world—
    men asking for their kind of love
    while mine is a kind of pinch-eyed drag of
going on, for that which seems so important to them
seems worthless to me.
so
I go back to the hotel room
and look at the pitcher of water on the dresser
and the bits of glass hung on string
left in the window by a Mexican whore
to reflect what's left of me
and this seems
sensible
as sensible as reading the history of the
Crimean War
as sensible as wax and women and
dogs.
I watch a fly and read the newspaper
then eat sausage and bananas
and an orange.

then I pull the shade on the speechmakers.
over the back of a chair are my
belt and necktie,
necktie knotted
for my throat
which is like a flower 80 feet high and
pumping out phrases of
bedlam.

mutilated forever at the age of
46. our dear sweet father said we'd come to
this.

a drawer of fish

he kept drawing fish
on sheets of paper
and I said,
Jack, what's wrong?
but he wouldn't answer
and his wife said
he won't look for a job
that's what's wrong,
and I gotta stay with
the kids; I don't know
how in the hell we're
going to make it.

he kept drawing fish
on sheets of paper
and he wasn't even drunk.

I went down and got 2
bottles of wine
and the old lady poured
them around.

and Jack drank his,
then cursed: this g.d.
ballpoint pen always runs
out of blood
just when I'm at the point,
the crux, just when I'm
finally burning
in the imbecile wax of fire . . .

he threw the pen
into a papersack full of empty bottles,
empty sardine and
bean cans, put on his coat
and walked out.

where's he going?
I asked.

I don't give a damn
where's he's going,
his old lady said.
then she pulled her dress back
and showed me a lot of leg;
it looked pretty good, I
have always been a leg man
but I walked over to the closet
and put on my coat.

where you going? she asked.

I'm going to look for a job,
I told her,
there's an ad in the Times,
they need janitors for the
new Fleischman building.

I walked down the steps
and half a block North
to the nearest bar.

Jack was sitting there.

I don't know, he said,
I think I'm going
to kill myself.

it doesn't matter, I said,
it's going to happen
anyhow.

we sat there the rest of the afternoon
drinking
and about 7 p.m. we left,
he with one with fire in her hair
and I with one with a limp
a reader of Henry James
who laughed out of the side
of her mouth.

it was 63 degrees
and not much left
of the world.

L. Beethoven, half-back

he came out for the team;
Ludwig V. Beethoven, blocking
half-back. he really knocked
them down. but he drank beer
and played the piano all night.
Schiller, you're a freak, he
said. leave the ladies alone.
the ladies will always be the
same. don't fret, when you
need one, she'll be there.

and Tchaikovsky, he said,
take some vitamins. I don't
mind that you're a homo:
just stay away
from me. that's the trouble
with all you guys:
you're too
pale!

I took a lateral from G. B. Shaw
and ducked around the end;
Beethoven blocked out 3 men,
and as I went past
he said, I got a couple of
babes lined up for tonight;
don't injure
anything
you might need
later . . .

I shot up the field
evading tacklers
like a madman. B. was
studying harmony, but
I doubted if he could
ever
make it. he was just
a fat
beer-drinking
German.

self-destruction

my snake's red fingers
he said
and they took him off the couch
and put him on the stretcher
and carried him down
25 steps
and his woman crossed her legs
(I could almost see her beautiful crotch)
and lit a cigarette
and said
I just
can't *kaant* see what possessed him,
and I slapped her across the face
flying the cigarette to the rug
like some Mars thing
and followed the stretcher
on down.

these mad windows that taste life and cut me if I go through them

I've always lived on second and third floors or higher
all my life
but I got some woman pregnant
and since she wasn't my wife
we moved over here—
we were in the back at first
2nd floor rear
as Mr. and Mrs.—
a new start—
and there was a madwoman in this
place and she kept the shades drawn
and hollered obscenities in the dark
(I thought she was pretty sharp)
but they took her away one day
and we moved in here and had the baby,
a beautiful skunk of a child with pale blue eyes
who made me swallow my heart like a cherry in a
        chilled drink,
but the woman decided I was insane too
and moved the child and herself to Hollywood
and I give them what money I can—
but most of the time I lay around all day
sweating in bed
wondering how much longer I can fool them
listening to my landlord outside
watering his lawn
46 years hanging on my bones
and big green tears cascade ha, ha,
down my face and are tabulated by my dirty pillow:
all those years shot through the head

assassinated forever
drunk senseless
hobbled and slugged in factories
poked with bad dreams
dripping away in mouse- and ghost-infested rooms
across an America without meaning,
boy o boy.

about 3 p.m. I get up
having failed to sleep but more than a few minutes
anyhow
and then I put on an old undershirt
crisp fresh torn shorts
and a pair of stolen army pants
and I pull up the shades
and sit a little back in a hard folding chair
near a window on the streetside
and then they come by,
young girls
fresh fluid divine intelligent
drinks of orange juice
rides in air-conditioned elevators,
in blue and green and yellow in motion
in red in waves
in squads and battalions of laughter
they laugh at me and for me,
old 46, at attention, pig green eyes
like a Van Gogh bursting and breaking
the trachea and tits of the earth and the sun,
my god, look, here I am
and no matter what I said to them
they would run away
I would be reported as an old goof
babbling in the marketplace for hard pennies—
they expect me to use the bathroom,
a shadow-picture for their singing flesh

and the pliers of my hand—
a good citizen jacksoff, votes, and looks at Bob Hope—
and even old maids
with husbands killed
making swivel chairs in industry
they walk by
in green in yellow in red
and they have bodies like high-school girls
they perch on their stilts and dare me to break
custom

but to have any of these would take weeks and months
of torture—introduction, niceties, conversation that
cleaves the soul like a rusty axe—
no, no, god damn it! no more!

a man who cannot adjust to society is called a
psychotic, and the boy in the Texas tower
who shot 49 and killed 15 was one,
although in the Marine Corps he got the o.k.
to go ahead—it's all in the way you're dressed
and if the beehive says the project
protects the Queen and Goodyear Rubber and so
forth,
but the way I see it from this window
his action was nothing extraordinary or
unexpected and psychiatrists are just paid liars
of a continuing social
disorder.

and soon I get up from the window
and move around
and if I turn on the radio
and luck on Shostakovich or Mahler
or sit down to type a letter to the president,
the voices begin all around me—

"HEY! KNOCK IT OFF!"
"YOU SON OF A BITCH! WE'LL CALL THE LAW!"

on each side of me are two high-rise apartments
things lit at night with blue and green lights
and they have swimming pools that everybody has
too much class to get into
but the rent is very high
and they sit looking at their walls
decorated with pictures of people with chopped-off
heads
and wait to go back to
WORK,
meanwhile, they sense that my sounds are not
their sounds—
66 people on each side of my head
in love with Green Berets and piranhas—
"GOD DAMN YOU, COOL IT!"

these I cannot see through my window
and for this I am glad
my stomach is in bad shape from drinking cheap wine,
and so for them
I become quiet
I listen to their sounds—
their baseball games, their comedies, their quiz shows,
their dry kisses, their kindling safety,
their hard bodies stuffed into the walls and murdered,
and I go to the table
take my madman's crayons
and begin drawing them on my walls
all of them—
loving, fucking, eating, shitting,
frightened of Christ, frightened of poverty,
frightened of life
they crawl my walls like roaches

and I draw suns between them
and axes and guns and towers and babies
and dogs, cats, animals, and it becomes
difficult to distinguish the animal from the
other, and my whole body sweats, stinks,
as I tremble like a liar from the truth of things,
and then I drink some water, take off my clothing and
go to bed
where I will not sleep
first pulling down all the shades
and then waiting for 3 p.m.
my girls my ladies my way
with nothing going through and nothing coming in and
nothing going out, Cathedrals and Art Museums and
mountains wasted, only the salt of myself, some ants,
old newspapers, my shame, my shame
at not having
killed
(razor, carcrash, turpentine, gaspipe)
(good job, marriage, investments in the market)
what is left of
myself.

birth

I.

reading the Dialogues of Plato when the
doctor walks up and says

> do you still read that highbrow
> stuff? last time I read that I
> was in
> high school.

> I read it, I tell
> him.

> well, it's a girl, 9#, 3 oz. no trouble at
> all.

> shit. great. when can I see
> them?

> they'll let you know. good
> night.

II.

I sit down to Plato again. there are 4 people playing
cards. one woman has beautiful legs that she doesn't hide
and I keep looking at her legs until she covers them with a
blue sweater.

III.

I am called upstairs. they show me the thing through glass.
it's red as a boiled crab and tough. it will make
it. it will see it through.

    hey, look at this, Plato: *another broad!*
I can see her now on some Sunday afternoon
shaking it in a tight skirt
making boulevards of young men warble in their
guts.

I wave the girl and the nurse
away.

IV.

the woman is still stunned with
drugs but I tell her

    a great woman has arrived!
and make my fists into little balls and I
hold up my arms and
snarl-cry.

the nurse is fat and Mexican, has eaten too many
tortillas.

    nice to have met you, sweetheart, I
tell her.

V.

then I am back at the shack. I sit down and listen to
the bathtub drip.

I go over and pull all the blinds down and fall on the
couch. all I can hear is tires on
steel streets.

VI.

there is a *meeow* from the screen and I let him
in: sober, indifferent,
hungry.

VII.

we walk into the kitchen
male, swaggering under the electric light;
4 balls, 2 heads
dominion over all the continent
over ships that sail in and out
over small female things and jewels.

I get down the can of
cat food and open
it. Plato is left in the
glove compartment.

on getting famous and being asked:
can you recite?
can you be there at nine?

   . . . and all they know is kill, these pungent insects,
and as we whirl in new worlds
I am filled with space and I
am ill; I roll a child's marble
upon the rug, then hear it
clatter off into some new corner
and I puke as the telephone rings;
MR. SPANISH, A VOICE SAYS, WE WANT
YOU TO SPEAK BEFORE THE
SOCIETY. WE FEEL IT WILL BE
VITAL. I hang up, of course,
and I find an orange
in the icebox, but before
I can peel it and eat it
I am ill again.
and
I take off
and fold my shoes, sit down cross-
legged, (like a statue I wish I
owned), and wait, at 3 p.m.,
to die.

the great one:

down at the end of the bar
he used to bum
drinks, now he is a balding man and
I lean close:
    you are the finest poet
    of our age, you are the
    only one that everybody
    understands . . .

we drink coffee, we sit in his small
poorly furnished house, his oil paintings
are on the walls. I am going to give him
money, paper, paint, a better
typewriter. he is going to give me some
original
manuscripts.

I look at him and sense that he fears
me. he coughs, his stomach must feel
oily, dense,
ill.

I tell him:
    I know all about you:
    you had a cruel Spanish
    stepfather, you lived with
    numerous whores, drank yourself
    senseless,
    starved . . .

yeah, he
says.

I lean closer:
 in my own quiet way,
 I am a worshipper of
 heroes . . .

when I leave with his manuscripts (signed)
and one of his oils plus
3 wire-coiled and unreadable
notebooks
he doesn't come to the door with me. there is a
mirror and he sits looking into the
mirror and he
bows his head, ashamed and
finished.

"The Artist," an ancient sage had once said,
"is always sitting on the doorsteps of the
rich."

I swing into my caddy, throw the junk in the
   back and
drive off.

yellow

Seivers was one of the hardest running backs since
Jimmy Brown, and lateral motion too,
like a chorus girl, really, until one day he got hit on
the blind side by Basil Skronski; we carried Seivers off the
        field
but Skronski had gotten one rib and cracked another.

the next year Seivers wasn't even good in practice, gun shy
        as a
squirrel in deer season; he stopped contact, fumbled, couldn't
        even
hold a look-in pass or a handoff—all that wasted and he
        could go the 100 in 9.7.

I'm 45 years old, out of shape, too much beer, but one of
        the best
assistant coaches in the pro game, and I can't stand to see a
        man
jaking it. I got him in the locker room the other day when
        the whole
squad was in there. I told him, "Seivers, you used to be a
        player
but now you're chickenshit!"

"you can't talk that way to me, Manny!" he said, and I
        turned him
around, he was lacing on a shoe, and I right-cracked him
right on the chin. he fell against a locker
and then he began to cry—the greatest since Brown,
crying there against the locker, one shoe off, one on.

"come on, men, let's get outa here!" I told the gang, and
        we ran
on out, and when we got back he had cleared out, he was
        gone, his
gear was gone. we got some kid from Illinois running his
        spot now,
head down, knees high, he don't care where's he's going.

guys like Seivers end up washing dishes for a buck an hour
and that's just what they deserve.

: : : *the days run away like wild horses over the hills*

the phone rings and it is usually the woman with the
sexy voice from the phone company telling me
to please pay my phone bill,
but this time a voice says quietly,
"you son of a bitch,"
and it is the editor of a dozen magazines,
everything from religious pamphlets
to do-it-yourself abortions,
and he asks,
"why haven't you called?"
and I say, "we don't get along."
"catalysis," he says,
"dig?"
"dig," I say,
and then he tells me that he has seen me
in issue No. 5 of *Crablegs and Muletears*
and that I am getting better,
and I tell him that I am a slow starter
and being only 42
I still stand a chance to spread sand
in Abdulah's garden,
and he says come on over
I want you to meet a friend
and I tell him I will give him a ring
after the track . . .

it is Saturday and hot
and the faces of greed rushing past
pinched and dried and impossible
want to make me kneel amongst the lilies and pray

but instead I go to a bar
where I can get good vodka and orange for 70¢
and people keep talking to me,
it is one big lonely hearts club,
people lonely for a voice and a million dollars
and not getting much of either,
and by the 9th race I am one hundred dollars in the hole
and a big colored guy walks up to me
and spreads the tickets of the last winner in his hand
like violin music,
and I say
"fine, fine,"
and he says, "I am with a couple of old broads
and now they are trying to find me,
but I am ducking out, I am going to lock the doors
and get drunk."
"fine," I say, and he walks off
and I keep wondering why so many colored people
talk to me, and then I remembered
I was in a bar once and a big black guy swore me into
something called the Muslims;
I had to repeat a lot of fancy words and
we drank all night,
but I thought he was kidding:
I am not out to destroy all the white race—
only a small part of it:
myself.

"who you like?" another guy asks me
and I say "the 3rd horse," and he says
"the 3 is out," and walks off
and that is all I want to hear
and I put 20 to win on the 3,
get a screwdriver
and walk down to the last turn
where if you've been around long enough

you can pick out the winner
before the stretch drive begins.
and I'm there when the 3 drives past
a length and a half behind the 6,
the others are out,
and it looks close, both are running hard
without signs of tiring
but I have to close the gap
and I look up at the board and see that
the 6 is 25-1 and I am only 7-1
and with a little luck I might make it,
and I did by three-quarters of a length
and the frogs of my mind lined up and
jumped over death (for a little while)
and I walked over and got my $166.

I was in the tub with a beer when the phone rang,
"bastard, where are you?"
it was the editor.
"see you in 30 minutes," I told him.
"I don't want any stuff outa you or I'll lay
you out," he tells me.
"fine," I say, "30 minutes then."
which gives me time for a couple more beers.

the place is in the back in South Hollywood,
a small cell with a water heater
in the bathroom, and a rack of books take up
half the room: much Huxley (Aldous), Lawrence
(not of Arabia), and a lot of tomes and vessels
of people halfway in the playground
between poetry and the novel
and lacking either the motivation or the discipline
to write straight philosophy,
and he had a woman in there

in the last peach fuzz of her youth,
pale orange, a little spiritless,
but quiet, which was good,
and he said, "baby, get the man a beer,"
and I threw him my latest book
which I inscribed, "to a connoisseur
of vagina and verse . . ."
and he said, "you are getting fat, bastard,
but you are looking better than the last time
I saw you."
"was that in Paris?" I asked.
"Pasadena, Calif.," he answered.
"Faulkner's dead now too," I said.
"how do you like the bitch?" he asked,
"look at her."
I looked at her and thanked her for the beer.
"fair stand the fields of France,"
I said.
"I need a hundred and a half," he told me.
"Jesus," I answered,
"I was just gonna ask you for the same thing."
"I hear Harry is back with his old lady."
"yeah. looking for a job. painting furniture. baby-sitting.
he was even a bartender one night."
"Harry? a *bartender?*"
"just for 3 hours. then he said he got tired."
"tired?"
" 'tired' is the word he used."
"I need a hundred and a half."
"who the hell doesn't?"
"Faulkner doesn't," he said.
"I wonder what he mixed in his drinks? I've got to slow
down . . ."

the bitch had some poems she wrote and I read them
and they were not bad considering that she was built for

other things, and the rest of the night was fairly dull,
no fist fights, too old to tango, tiger asleep in the shade,
and I promised I would write an essay ON THE MEANING
    OF
MODERN POETRY which he promised to print unseen
and which I knew I would never write.
the night was full of promises, an old tiger
and a peach. I drove home down the side streets,
swinging wide around the police station,
smoking king-sized and humming parts from *Carmen*
because it was very dark and Bizet drove better than
Ludwig who had his mind on more important things.

I parked out in front and no sooner did I get the car door
    open
than the rummy downstairs said,
"hey, ace, how about a cold one?"
I took a beer out of the bag and slipped it in through the
    screen.
"I need a dollar," he said.
"now, ain't that a bitch? I was just gonna ask you for the
    same thing."
"you're in a bad mood," he said.
"sure," I said, "haven't you heard? Faulkner's dead."
"Faulkner? wasn't he a bullring jock? Pomona Fairgrounds?
Rudioso? Caliente? you knew the kid?"
"I knew the kid," I said
and then walked on upstairs.

the rest of the night was no-account, as the Arkies say,
and there were a couple of numbers I could dial,
4 or 5 numbers, some black, some white,
some old, some young,
but I kept thinking of white hospitals
and palm trees in the shade,
and it was quiet, at last it was quiet,

and there are times when you have to come back
and look around, there are times of Ludwig,
there are times of walls,
there are times of thinking of Ernest
and that shotgun raised to his head;
there are times for thinking
of dead loves, dead flowers,
of all the dead, dead people who give you a name,
from Florida to Del Mar, Calif.,
all the sadness like a parade
of gentle fools gone,
water running in sinks,
stockings washed,
gowns worn, thrown away,
the ugly duckling world
quietly slipping away from me
and myself slipping away,
an old tiger,
sick of the battle.

the next morning I was awakened by a knock on the door,
so I ignored it, I never answer the door,
I don't want to see anybody,
but it kept up with a kind of gentle persistence
so I got up and put on my old yellow robe
dead voices from bedrooms
and opened the door.
"I am here to help the handicapped people," she said.
"do come in," I said.
she was a young girl 19, 20, 21,
her eyes as innocent as the map of Texas spread
over the clouds,
and she walked across the rug and sat down
and I went into the kitchen and took the cap
off of 2 beers. my goldfish swam like crazy.
I walked out with the beers, I said,

"love must be always
because stones gone flat with leaning
take ships to sea
take cats and dogs and
everything."

she laughed and the day began without
error.

worms

a guy told me,
you don't have to worry about worms when you're
dead
they never get to you
the body changes like in all different
ways—by the time
they've worked through the casket
things have happened and it
always happens
different—
they've dug up these old kings outa tombs, ya
know:
one guy was just
a little splotch of black
water, another had a
beard 18 feet long and another had
turned to a kind of rock-like
salt.

yeah? I said.
yeah, he said.

he knew *all* these things.
he lived high in the hills and had these
tremendous brains.

before I left I reached out and
pulled the worms out of his
eyes nose belly shoes hair ears
and then he said

good night
and I said
good night
and I got in my car and drove off

and the worms laughed
all the way home.

to hell with Robert Schumann

I finished my drink and went back
upstairs to hear the second half—
another piano concerto, and
2 are too many and
I couldn't make it out
having lost my program so
I left the place and drove 21 blocks
South and East
to where 2 flyweights
a Jap and a Mexican were
going at it. the
Mexican butted the Jap and
the Jap bled from a cut
above the eye
but only fought harder
he was grasshopper slim with
very thin arms but
hit very hard. it went all ten and
the Jap got the verdict. another
ten followed. I drank a lot of
beer
kept leaving to piss and
when I came back one time it
was over: k.o.,
and I walked out to my car and
since I was downtown I
drove to where I worked in the
daylight
to see if maybe the place looked less
painful and
I looked through the window and

thought I saw Ralph the stockboy in
there
crawling around on his hands and his
knees. he was an odd one and
the secretaries were afraid of him
and I thought I should call the
police
but then I thought
I don't care if he raids the
place or sets it on
fire. I got back into my car
and took the freeway back to my
apartment.

I drank a couple glasses of scotch,
set the clock for 6:30
ate a vitamin
thought about a whore in Glendale
checked the ball scores
pissed again
turned out the lights
got into bed (alone)
didn't pray
thought of places like Japan and
Central Avenue
thought about the dead and
the famous
thought about dying
while the Thames went along without
me and the girls walked up and down the
sidewalks without me
and then I thought I wouldn't mind
so much
and went to sleep and
slept good.

the seminar

(dedicated to my betters)

Wednesday, 24 July 1969; Morning Session (Robert Hansen
and Allen Truport):
> discussed sure discussed

WORK HABITS. Bob ingests, ingests, ingests, so we get those
wonderfully turned—
> Allen keeps large notebooks
> wherein
>> he told us

he notes down EVERYTHING. a kind of spatial flowing
viewPOINT.
Allen says
> he writes all the time as much as possible;
> it's like hanging a coat in a closet: you've
> got to get in there. reasonableness may not be
> enchanting, but said Allen, it is REWARDING.

a big notebook, he said, by God that's the
> THING!

> like Genet on the sand
>> blowing cock!

Bob said:
> what the primary interest is and should be is ingesting,

ingesting, a kind of pulmonary percussion indrawn, tightened
> and

then placed upon the paper, the marble in tight order of grip,
allowing the function to be the (possible) anguish rather than
> any
>> MESSAGE or a) art-order
>>> b) audience-relationship.

163

Allen: I want to write
                    ENOUGH POEMS
                                        so that when I die
all the shit will be out of me, I mean the guff, the nonsense,
the turds yes, ah I mean—that I have expressed enough
ENOUGH you see to
                            free me.
R.H.—I realize the standard essence of all your POETRY;
I say content is an extension of form. we must barter
        for a firmer divinity. the conduct of children,
for instance, is fairly free but
UNFORMED
                    and in the final
multiplication . . . useless.
        I would say that the difference between
Hansen and Truport is that Hansen KNOWS
what he is
            doing.
Evening Session (R.H. and A.T.)
Bob says priests should stick to their robes and leave
        POETRY
                    to him.
I agree
        with this.
Allen says political poetry or poetry dealing with immediate
        causes and reflections is
                            interesting, and interesting
                            goes well, badly written
or not, it appears IMPORTANT, is appears sympathetic
and the ONE THING I do not want to do is lose
                                    my AUDIENCE.

Thursday, July 25th; no classes:
                    a dozen of us had gone over to Buchanan 106

164

for the hell of

       it

             to use the lecture room
              anyhow
but we found some WOMEN in there
and they appeared HOSTILE when we walked in and
even MORE hostile when we began talking about

                 POETRY.
their hostility is perhaps understandable because we
       DON'T

          tend to them.
they'll just have to WAIT until workshop

         CLASSES to get a portion of our
attention.

    but it was really something, all of us there together,
talking, TALKING,—Hansen, Truport, Missions, De Costro
Sevadov, and Starwort, all all

         together

           here in ONE room was
the heart of American POETRY

      talking, my

        god.

Friday, July 26th; Morning Session:
    De Costro dominated the whole damned meeting. he has
    big hands and many

       IDEAS. Truport appears to be afraid
of De Costro. Hansen cools it. nobody gets along.
yet there is no

    YELLING. these are *only* poets.
De Costro says the root of the thing is transferred to the tree
and the tree dies and

    becomes HISTORY

      and that

        generally

history is pretty
                    disappointing, it's easier to chop down a
tree than a poem, he says, history chops
                    YOU down.
FUCK ALL MEANING! Bob suddenly screams.
then, in softer voice:
                    we ought to *discard*.
we all agree that feeling is *everything* and
                    we go out for coffee
                              leaving three girls sitting
there with their dresses hiked-up around their
                                        HIPS.

Monday, July 29th; Morning Session:

    I saw all FIVE OF THEM! ! !
                              around a desk
                                   TOGETHER:
                                   Hansen, Truport,
                                   De Costro,
                                   Starwort and
                                   Phillip Maxwell.
Phillip didn't ARGUE didn't say much
and left before the meeting was OVER
                                   but explained he'd wait
OUTSIDE for the free lunch. his books haven't been
                              GOING well.
Starwort read his *Man on a Streetcar Running Backwards*
                    from *Bent Lily* #8.
I couldn't really understand his
                    READING
                              but will have to see
the work in print before I make a
                    JUDGMENT.

Maybe Allie Denby
will send me a
copy of the issue, tho, alas, I understand it is
now a RARE ITEM
going to $20 out of Fort Lauderdale.
the past can only take place in the PRESENT, if you
know what I mean, said
De Costro.
we all
nodded.
Truport said he was afraid of being BROKE. he was
lined up for one more session at the
U. of K.
but hadn't heard much
more. of course, he'd been moving
around quite a bit, in TOUCH and
OUT OF TOUCH:
Paris, Cuba, the Congo, India, Moscow and Denver, Colorado.
we spoke of *The Cantos*.
Pound continually tries to find space
AREAS, ARENAS OF CONTOUR for his extra-cerebral
power-poetic
uningrained . . . uncontrived soul-mind . . . like a . . . like a
whip lashing against the sides of an old
BARN.
we want a COMPLETE EMERGENCE, said De Costro.
nothing half   nothing wilted
we want the poetic Christ-thing walking out of
the barn
and Teaching—not from the TOP-down
but through and through and
THROUGH.

god damn it to hell, said Starwort. suddenly.
in taking my notes I could not fit it into

the
conversation.

First Workshop session with R.H.:
he seemed to say a lot that I didn't understand but
the others seemed to understand
and the session went well.
Bob looked well. I had a
HANGOVER.

Wednesday, July 31st; Morning Session (most of us there):

there were again the old arguments about Vietnam,
Cleaver and the Panthers, all of which, I am afraid, I
no longer
understand.
I am AFRAID
I am getting tired
although the others appear very
energetic.
I need SECURITY, said Hansen. I need a perpetual FATHER
and a GOOD JOB or my work is
HINDERED.
Allen read some of his early stuff. I understand some of it
but FRANKLY, I think he tends to
holler and OVERSTAGE.
I left with a
HEADACHE.

Friday, August 2nd; Morning Session:

Allen spoke of some of the poetry he had seen in
the campus shithouses and said it was pretty
GOOD.
then Wm. Burroughs was discussed

168

his USE of timely and pertinent
news material that RELATED . . .

by clipping out words in the paper
and pasting them in DIFFERENT ORDER
A NEW ORDER

was established
and a neutralization of time and event
WAS

established.
THIS WAs imporTANT. YeS. I'll sAY sO.
we all admitted we often read *Time* and

Pravda.
then Allen read
AGAIN

this time from UnpubliSHED
WoRk
dIrEcTly FrOM the JOuRnals

there were 250 people attending
and he read LOUDLY and I had another
HANGOVER.
he screamed for FORTYFIVE MINUTES! then became
TERRIBLY
exhausted, you couldn't hear him, his voice BECAME
a monotonous drone and he asked the audience:
may I stop now?
they applauded LOUDLY.

Sunday, August 4th:

the janitor had locked all the doors on the campus so
we met at Hansen's room and drank port wine. Denise and
Carol came up but they were SAFE
although everyone appeared a little sullen.
I think it was being LOCKED OUT like that.
later in the night Allen grew angry and slapped

Bob. then Allen read his poetry again. it was
    good   being there   all together   all of us.
I have tried to take notes and hope you have
                     APPRECIATED THEM.
next summer I am sure we will be
                     INVITED BACK
and I look forward
         EAGERLY
                 to these great American poets
and their DISCUSSION of what makes POETRY GO, what it
iS! !
     AnD To haVE tHem rEaD thEiR OWN WORKS OnCe
     AgAin.

                      —*Howard Peter, University of L.*
                               August 5, 1969

one for Ging, with klux top

I live among rats and roaches
but there is this high-rise apt., a new one
across from me, glimmering pool, lived in by very young
people with new cars, mostly red or white cars,
and I allow myself to look upon this scene as
some type of miracle world
not because it is possibly so
but because it is easier to think this way,
—why take more knives?—
so today I sat here and I saw one young man
sitting in his red car
sucking his thumb and waiting
as another young man, obviously his friend,
talked to a young woman dressed in kind of long slim short
pants, yes, and a black ill-fitting blouse,
and she had on some kind of high-pointed hat, rather
like the kukluxklan wear, and the other young man sucked,
     sat and
    sucked his thumb
    in the
red car and
behind them, through the glass door
the other young people sat and sat and sat and sat
around the blue pool,
and the young woman was angry
she was ugly anyhow and now she was very ugly
but she must have had something to interest the young man
and she said something violent and final
(I couldn't hear any of it)
and walked off west, away from the young man and the
    building,

and the young man was flushed in the face, seemingly more
        stunned
than angry, and then they both sat in the car for a while,
and then the other young man took his thumb out of his
mouth, and started the red car, and then they were
gone.

and through my window and through the glass door
I could see the other young people
sitting sitting sitting
around the blue pool. my miracle crowd, my future
leaders.

to make it round out, I decided that the night before
the young man (not the one with the thumb) had tried
to screw the ugly girl in the pointed hat while they were both
drunk, and that the ugly girl in the pointed hat
felt—for some reason—that this was a damned dirty trick.
she acted bit parts in little theatre—was said to have talent—
had a fairly wealthy father, and her name was Gig or
        Ging or
something odd like that—and that was mainly why the boys
        wanted to
screw her: because her first name was Gig or Ging
        or Aszpupu,
and the boys wanted to say, very much wanted to say:
"I balled with Ging last night."

all right, so having settled all that,
I put on some coffee and rolled myself something
calming.

communists

we ran the women in a straight line down to the river
clinging to the fear in their rice-stupid heads
clinging to their infants
mice-like sucklings breathing in the air at odds of
one thousand to one;
we shot the men as they kneeled in a circle,
and the death of the men held almost no death,
it was somehow like a movie film,
men of spider arms and legs and a hunk of cloth
to cover the sexual organ.
men hardly born could hardly be killed
and there they were down there now, finally dead,
the sun straining on their faces of weird
puzzlement.

some of the women could fire rifles. we left a small
detachment to decide upon
them. then we fired up the unburned huts and moved on
to the next village.

family, family

I keep looking at the
kid
up
    side
        down,
and I am tickling
her sides
as her mother pins new
diapers
on,
    and the kid doesn't look like
    me
uʍopǝpᴉsdn—
    so I get ready to
kill them both
       but
    relent:

I don't even
look like
    myself—
        rightsideup, so.
shit on it!
I tickle again, say
crazy
    words, and and and and
hope
    all the while
that this
    very unappetizing
world

174

does not blow up
in all our
        laughing
faces.

poem for the death of an American serviceman in Vietnam:

shot through a hole in the
bellybutton
9 miles wide—
    out it came:
    those Indian head pennies
    those old dead whores
    the sick sea walking like
pink
    toast
past bottles of orange
    children
dripping
    drip
       dry

barometer
    lowering
while the guns elevated like
    erections—
tossed the apple salad back
into the
    sky.

(he died then, stuffing balloons with
marbles as the prince
laughed.)

guilt obsession behind a cloud of rockets:

genuinely traginew, dandy then, babe,
the age-old bile:
dummies stuffed with wax and
steel,
a deeper dark than any dark
we have ever
known—
I do not speak of such obvious things as
skin—
christ, it's a bad
fix, ghostly true,
I might even say
off the top of the bottle
that I suffer more than
most, haha, but
I've also found that
good men
neither talk about their virtues or
their possibilities,
—strike deep here,
catch fish, headaches, sores, blisters,
traffic tickets, tooth decay, hatred from
lesbians, the surgeon's brown
finger—
if death is so fearful
then life must be
good?
dandy then, babe, genuinely
traginew, and
I've found out why men
sign their names to their

works—
not that they created them
but more
than the others did
not.

even the sun was afraid

they'd stuck him in the shoulder and
he came out
pissed—
feeling all the space of ground
feeling the sunshine
and
looking for somebody.

it stood there.

it seemed that even the sun was afraid of the
bull.

the matador screamed something
shook and flagged the cape.
the bull came at him.
he gave him the cap . but the mat did not get very
close.

then the bull saw the padded
horse, the blindfolded horse,
and he trotted over
and began working his horns against the horse's
side and underside.

the pic
there on top of the horse
lanced him good
he stuck him deep and hard with the
pole
really muscling it in

screwing it in deep
right in the top part of the back there
up near the neck.

this makes the bull go more for the horse—
he probably thinks the horse is doing it to him—
and as he goes more for the horse
he gets drilled more and more
by the chickenshit
lance.

the bull left the horse
went for the cape
then came back to the horse.
then he got another drilling by the
pic.

he does not any longer quite look like the
bull who first ran into the ring.
but they haven't cut him down enough
they have something else for
him: the banderillas.

short sharp pieces that are jammed into the upper back
and neck, the placement of these does *appear*
dangerous.
no cape is used and these young Mexican boys
stupid and with dirty
behinds
they leap into the air and make the
placements as the bull runs
by.

we watched them make the
placements.

now the bull was properly ready for the matador to be
brave.
the neck and back muscles were severed, shredded in
many places.
the head came
down.

Harry took a drink. "these Mexican bulls aren't any
good. you oughta see the Spanish bulls. they got horns
like this":
he showed me how they had horns like that. with his
hands. then we both had a
drink.

the matador did not seem to get in very
close. the bull kept getting in those
tired and desperate lunges at the cape
getting more and more winded
more and more
useless.

each of the matador's movements had some meaning, some
name. the Mexicans knew it. the drunken Americans in the
shade with good jobs and subnormal wives
didn't know anything. they rooted for the
bull.
they didn't know that it took guts
to even do a bad job with the bull.

well, this bull was bad and the matador was bad
but the matador was worse than the
bull, and I guess that's about as bad as the act can
get.
except when the bull is so much *less* worse than the
matador and the mat gets gored and the Americans go
home happy and

fuck all night
trying to forget about the job in the
morning.

kill time came. the mat knew what to do. he knew the
spot. it was like running a hot poker into a
barrel of loose tin foil.

the bull
beaten and stabbed about the neck and back
winded totally by ripping at a vision of a
red cape that only
gave, gave, gave
folded over the horn forever—
the bull was winded *spiritually* as
well.
and finally stood
disgusted and doomed
looking
LOOKING.

we had another
drink. we knew the plot, the hero, the whole
fucking thing. the sword went
in.

but it wasn't
over.
the bull stood there.
and with the sword cutting his vitals
they came up.

4 or 5 Mexicans with dirty
behinds. including the
mat.

and they turned
him. flicked their capes at
him. punched him on the
nose.

still he wouldn't
fall.
they were trying to push him into death
but he was hanging
in.

and every now and then
the head would remember
and give a lunge of
horn and
they would step back
remembering their own deaths.

then the mat came up
pulled the sword
out, stuck it home
again.

still no good.
the bull would not go
down.

we had another drink.

"you see," said Harry, "they keep turning him. that
sword is cutting him. every time they make him move,
the sword cuts again."

finally somebody took his foot and
kicked the bull over and the bull
fell down.

but still
it wasn't any
good.
the bull kept kicking his
legs, trying to get
up. he wouldn't
quit.

so then a little fat chap came
out. he was all dressed in white and wore a little
white butcher's cap. he seemed quite
angry.
he had a short blade and walked up
and very angry and quick
he chopped and chopped and chopped and
chopped. it appeared that he was chopping at the
bull's head, his
brain.

the bull couldn't get at the boy in the
butcher's cap. he had to
take it. finally one of the chops
took.

you could SEE the bull
die. the bull gave it
up. the crowd
cheered.

Harry took a
drink, that was the end of that
pint. and that
matador.

"what's the name of the next
bull?" I asked
Harry.

"I don't know. the light is
bad."

anyhow, the next bull came
out.

we had one more pint and the
drive back in.

on a grant

    . . . an ocean liner
the Captain smiles and farts and knows my
name
the sea is boiling and smells of
torn chunks and warm raw meat
    and
half-daft sick spiders try to
wind their dead legs around each other
around everything
but they tangle off slide off drift off
losing legs against the prow
and wanting to scream and not being able to
scream
    while
I am on the grant from a University
    and
translating Rimbaud and Lorca and
Günter Grass over and over
again
    then
after a conversation on Proust and
Patchen I rape a
rich beautiful girl in my cabin
    and
afterwards she turns into a
dead peach tree which I
hang on the wall
    then
I awaken in a small dirty bedroom and the
woman walks in:

"listen, I need a stroller. the kid is getting too heavy to carry."

"o.k., o.k."

"but when? when?"

"not today. too god damned tired."

"tomorrow?"

"tomorrow, sure."

finish

the hearse comes through the room filled with
the beheaded, the disappeared, the living
mad.
the flies are a glue of sticky paste
their wings will not
lift.
I watch an old woman beat her cat
with a broom.
the weather is unendurable
a dirty trick by
God.
the water has evaporated from the
toilet bowl
the telephone rings without
sound
the small limp arm petering against the
bell.
I see a boy on his
bicycle
the spokes collapse
the tires turn into
snakes and melt
away.
the newspaper is oven-hot
men murder each other in the streets
without reason.
the worst men have the best jobs
the best men have the worst jobs or are
unemployed or locked in
madhouses.
I have 4 cans of food left.

air-conditioned troops go from house to
house
from room to room
jailing, shooting, bayoneting
the people.
we have done this to ourselves, we
deserve this
we are like roses that have never bothered to
bloom when we should have bloomed and
it is as if
the sun has become disgusted with
waiting
it is as if the sun were a mind that has
given up on us.
I go out on the back porch
and look across the sea of dead plants
now thorns and sticks shivering in a
windless sky.
somehow I'm glad we're through
finished—
the works of Art
the wars
the decayed loves
the way we lived each day.
when the troops come up here
I don't care what they do for
we already killed ourselves
each day we got out of bed.
I go back into the kitchen
spill some hash from a soft
can, it is almost cooked
already
and I sit
eating, looking at my
fingernails.
the sweat comes down behind my

ears and I hear the
shooting in the streets and
I chew and wait
without wonder.

the underground

the place was crowded.
the editor told me,
"Charley get some chairs from upstairs,
there are more chairs upstairs."
I brought them down and we opened the beer and
the editor said,
"we're not getting enough advertising,
the boat might go down,"
so they started talking about how to get
advertising.
I kept drinking the beer
and had to piss
and when I got back
the girl next to me said,
"we ought to evacuate the city,
that's what we ought to do."

I said, "I'd rather listen to Joseph Haydn."

she said, "just *think* of it,
if everybody left the city!"

"they'd only be someplace else
stinking it up," I said.

"I don't think you like
people," she said, pulling her short skirt down
as much as possible.

"just to fuck with," I said.

then I went to the bar next door and
bought 3 more packs of beer.
when I got back they were talking Revolution.
so here I was back in 1935 again,
only I was old and they were young. I was at least
20 years older than anybody in the room,
and I thought, what the hell am I doing
here?

soon the meeting ended
and they went out into the night,
those young ones
and I picked up the phone, I got
John T.,
"John, you o.k.? I'm low tonight.
suppose I come over and get
drunk?"

"sure, Charley, we'll be waiting."

"Charley," said the editor, "I guess we've got to
put the chairs back
upstairs."

we carried the chairs back upstairs
the
revolution was
over.

from the Dept. of English

100 million Chinese bugs on the stairway to
hell,
come drink with me
rub my back with me;
this filth-pitched room,
floor covered with yellow newspapers
3 weeks old; bottle caps, a red
pencil, a rip of
toilet paper, these odd bits of
broken things;
the flies worry me as ice cream ladies
walk past my window;
at night I sleep, try to sleep
between mounds of stinking laundry;
ghosts come out,
play dirty games, evil games, games of horror with
my mind;
in the morning there is blood on the sheet
from a broken sore upon my
back.

putting on a shirt that rips across my
back, rotten rag of a thing,
and putting on pants with a rip in the
crotch, I find in the mailbox
(along with other threats):
"Dear Mr. Bukowski:
    Would like to see more of your poems for
    possible inclusion in
    —— Poetry Review.

How's it going?"

footnote upon the construction of the masses:

some people are young and nothing
else and
some people are old and nothing
else
and some people are in between and
just in between.

and if the flies wore clothes on their
backs
and all the buildings burned in
golden fire,
if heaven shook like a belly
dancer
and all the atom bombs began to
cry,
some people would be young and nothing
else and
some people old and nothing
else,
and the rest would be the same
the rest would be the same.

the few who are different
are eliminated quickly enough
by the police, by their mothers, their
brothers, others; by
themselves.

all that's left is what you
see.

it's
hard.

kaakaa & other immolations

wondrous, sure, kid, you want more
applejuice? how can you drink that goddamned
stuff? I hate it. what? no, I'm not Dr.
Vogel. I'm the daddy. your old man. where's mama?
she's out joining an artist's colony. oh, that's a place
where people go who aren't
artists. yes, that's the way it works almost
everywhere. sometimes you can go into a hospital and
it can be 40 floors high and there won't be a doctor in
there, and hard to find a nurse either.
what's a hospital? a hospital is just a bunch of
disconnected buttons, dying people and very sophisticated and
comfortable orderlies. but the whole world is like this:
nobody knows what they are supposed to know—
poets can't write poetry
mechanics can't fix your car
fighters can't fight
lovers can't love
preachers can't preach. it's even like that with
armies: whole armies led without generals,
whole nations led without leaders, why the whole thing is like
trying to copulate with a wooden
dick . . . oh, pardon me!
how old are you? three? three. ah. three fingers, that's nice!
you learn fast, my little ducky. what? more
applejuice? o.k.
you wanna play train? you wanna take me for a ride?
o.k., Tucson, we'll go to Tucson, what the hell!
damn it, I don't KNOW if we're there yet, you're
driving!
what? we're on the way BACK already?

you want some candy? shit, you been eatin' candy for hours!
listen, I don't KNOW when your mother will be back, uh?
        well,
after signing up for the artist's colony she's going to a poetry
reading. what's a poetry reading? a poetry reading is where
people gather and read their poetry to each other, the ones
mostly who can't write poetry.
what's poetry? nobody knows. it changes. it works by itself
like a snail crawling up the side of a house. oh, that's a big
squashy thing that goes all gooey and slimy when you
        step on
it. am I a snail?
I guess so kid, what?
you wanna kaakaa?
o.k., go ahead. can you get your own pants down? I don't
        see
you very often. oh, you want the light on? you want me
        to stay
or go away? stay? fine, then.
now kaakaa, little one, that's it . . .
kaakaa . . .
so you can grow up to be a big woman and
do what big women
do.
kaakaa.
at's it, sweet,
ain't it *funny*?
mama kaakaa too.
oh *yeah*

wow!
that's all right!
now wipe your ass.
no, better than
that! there, that's
better.

you say *I'm* kaakaa!
hey that's
good! I like that!
very funny.

now let's go get some more beer and
applejuice.

a problem of temperament

I played the radio all night the night of the 17th.
and the neighbors applauded
and the landlady knocked on the door
and said
PLEASE
PLEASE
PLEASE
MOVE,
you make the sheets dirty
where does the *blood* come from?
you *never* work.
you lay around and talk to the radio
and drink
and you have a beard
and you are always smirking
and bringing those women
to your room
and you never comb your hair
or shine your shoes
and your shirts are wrinkled
why don't you *leave*?
you are making the neighbors
        unhappy,
please make us all happy
and go away!

go to hell, baby, I hissed through
the keyhole; mah rent's paid 'til
Wednesday. can I show you a watercolor
nude painted in 1887 by an unknown German

artist? I have it insured for
$1,000.

unrelenting, she stamped down the hall.
no *artiste,* she. I would
like to see her in the nude, though.
perhaps I could *paint* my way
to freedom. *no?*

poetess

For S.S.V.

she lived in a small room by the freeway and she
wrote like a man—somebody who worked on the dock
—and I tapped on her window and she let me in, I
climbed through the window and I sat down as the
stupid fingers of my mind reached around the room,
I told her I had been on a drunk and that I had to
cut my toenails (they hurt) and I told her that
there were a lot of people getting on my nerves like
a broken glove compartment and she walked over and
kissed me, asked if I wanted coffee and if I had
been eating, and then she told me her radio was brok-
en—she had dropped it on the floor. and I took a
knife blade and worked at the screws in the back.
            be careful, she said, it says
            there is danger of shock, and I told
            her: I am immortal, I can't get or
            be killed.

she set a cheese sandwich and a cup of coffee in
front of me and I straightened up the loose tubes,
there seemed to be no broken ones, but it was get-
ting to be time for the first race and I told her,
Jesus, I don't have time!
            if you're immortal, she said,
            you have plenty of time.

I ate the cheese sandwich and drank the coffee.
            see you tonight, I said, I'll
            put the god damned thing together
            tonight.

I climbed out the window and into my car. the sun
came down in the dust and dirt of the parking lot
making everything a good soft yellow and brown, and
the vines on the fence smelled green the way green
smells, and I drove out backing up, waving to her
through the windshield and she stood in the window
waving and smiling, and I backed up the alley and
around the street, put it in forward and ran
along the pavement toward the freeway, out of there,
thinking about what I had done or hadn't done to
the radio (or her), feeling as if I had left an
army in trouble during battle, but then some kid
in a Volks

        cut across me without a signal
        and I forgot about all the rest
        and I pushed the pedal down and
        moved after him.

the miracle

To work with an art form
does not mean to
screw off like a tapeworm
with his belly full,
nor does it justify grandeur
or greed, nor at all times
seriousness, but I would guess
that it calls upon the best men
at their best times,
and when they die
and something else does not,
we have seen the miracle of immortality:
men arrived as men,
departed as gods—
gods we knew were here,
gods that now let us go on
when all else says stop.

Mongolian coasts shining in light

Mongolian coasts shining in light,
I listen to the pulse of the sun,
the tiger is the same to all of us
and high   oh
so high on the branch
our oriole
sings.

PHOTO: Sam Cherry

CHARLES BUKOWSKI is one of America's best-known contemporary writers of poetry and prose, and, many would claim, its most influential and imitated poet. He was born in Andernach, Germany, to an American soldier father and a German mother in 1920, and brought to the United States at the age of three. He was raised in Los Angeles and lived there for fifty years. He published his first story in 1944 when he was twenty-four and began writing poetry at the age of thirty-five. He died in San Pedro, California, on March 9, 1994, at the age of seventy-three, shortly after completing his last novel, *Pulp* (1994).

During his lifetime he published more than forty-five books of poetry and prose, including the novels *Post Office* (1971), *Factotum* (1975), *Women* (1978), *Ham on Rye* (1982), and *Hollywood* (1989). Among his most recent books are the posthumous editions of *What Matters Most Is How Well You Walk Through the Fire* (1999), *Open All Night: New Poems* (2000), *Beerspit Night and Cursing: The Correspondence of Charles Bukowski and Sheri Martinelli, 1960-1967* (2001), and *Night Torn Mad with Footsteps: New Poems* (2001), *sifting through the madness for the Word, the line, the way: New Poems* (2003), and *The Flash of Lightning Behind the Mountain* (2004).

All of his books have now been published in translation in over a dozen languages and his worldwide popularity remains undiminished. In the years to come Ecco will publish additional volumes of previously uncollected poetry and letters.